HITTING *the* GROUND RUNNING

J. R. GALE

Copyright © 2023 J. R. Gale
All rights reserved
First Edition

Fulton Books
Meadville, PA

Published by Fulton Books 2023

ISBN 979-8-88982-478-7 (paperback)
ISBN 979-8-88982-480-0 (digital)

Printed in the United States of America

To Mom, because she told me to and for her endless love and support. I wouldn't be who I am without her.

CONTENTS

Chapter 1 1
Chapter 2 13
Chapter 3 22
Chapter 4 29
Chapter 5 40
Chapter 6 45
Chapter 7 52
Chapter 8 57
Chapter 9 63
Chapter 10 71
Chapter 11 76
Chapter 12 83
Chapter 13 90
Chapter 14 97
Chapter 15 103
Chapter 16 106
Chapter 17 112
Chapter 18 117
Chapter 19 125
Chapter 20 131
Chapter 21 138
Chapter 22 149
Chapter 23 157
Chapter 24 163
Chapter 25 168
Chapter 26 177

Chapter 27 186
Chapter 28 192
Chapter 29 195
Chapter 30 202

CHAPTER 1

"Alright, pick a seat, and then we'll just talk, alright?" The rain pattered on the window, like tears streaking down a pale solemn face. I looked between the chairs. One was blue, its cushioning well-worn in, comforting, and next to the large window. The other was red, hard, and new, yet shiny and held a clean slate.

"Karissa?" the therapist nudged. "Is something wrong?"

I felt uneasiness grow in my stomach. *Is something wrong?* Her words replayed in my head over and over. Each syllable bounced through my skull like a bell. I slumped in the blue chair and didn't reply.

She settled with her clipboard in her lap and slipped on her large metal-framed glasses. "Alright, sweetie, let's chat."

Again, I looked out the window. People rushed down their streets, hidden under their cliché black umbrellas. Something about the rain had always reminded me of funerals, which led to the harsh reality of why I was sitting here today. Blinking rapidly, I turned back to Mrs. Blaine.

She gave a patient smile. "So, Karissa, what brings you here?"

"I'm not sure," I admitted, the persistent rasp of my voice refusing to ever leave. "I've been putting this off for a long time."

"And why do you think that is?"

Why did I not want to come? Maybe because I wasn't ready to relive it. To watch it all happen again, to feel it all happen again. "It's just been so chaotic since…" My words faded and died.

"Is there something you *would* like to talk about?"

I noticed the tissues in her garbage, bundled and tossed after being used. "What do you mean?"

She leaned back in her armchair, pushing the excessive amount of throw pillows over the side. "Well, the first session can be…overwhelming in a way. I don't want to overwhelm you since it was such a big step to come in the first place. Let's start simple. So, Karissa, were you close with your family?"

"Yes." From the consistent cheerful look plastered on her face, I knew she wanted me to go on, but I didn't give in.

"And how many siblings did you have?"

I paled and shook my head, my tears dripping off my eyelashes and onto the wrinkled blue rug.

"Alright, alright." Mrs. Blaine held up her hands. "We don't have to talk about them."

I looked at the picture of her family on the end table. Her husband carried a young girl on his shoulders, and she held two little boys' hands. Their smiles were almost contagious. "I had three siblings. My twin, Matt, and the younger twins, Taylor and Tyler."

"Two sets of twins?" she said in joyous shock. "Your poor parents."

A taxi honked on the street below, tearing me from my constant gaze at her photo. "My dad left right before Matt and I's fourteenth birthday, so it was just my mom."

"Well, she's a hero for raising four kids alone," she commended.

I just shrugged, watching the taxi peel away, throwing the finger as he left. "She worked a lot for us."

As an awkward feeling settled over the room, she shook her head and leaned forward. "So what was your favorite thing to do growing up?"

That was an easy answer. "Dance."

Mrs. Blaine seemed excited just by the fact that I had answered. "You danced?" She almost cheered. "For how long?"

"Fifteen years," I proudly, yet quietly, admitted. "I started when I was two years old."

"That's loyal, Karissa," she said soothingly.

"Taylor started dancing when she was that age too," I added, not sure why. "She had the same passion for it."

"What did dance mean to you?"

I wanted to close my eyes to feel the dance again, but instead, I looked at the hole in my sneakers. "Everything."

*****

Madame Roussel clapped her hands angrily. "*Non*," she snapped in her thick accent. "Do it again, now."

My back screamed at me as I picked myself up from the floor, my feet threatened to bleed from the blisters. I bit back a snarky comment and repositioned myself in front of the mirrors.

"You know where to start," she said, placing herself on my left.

My feet were in the fifth position; I raised my arms and became the music. I spun myself around again and again. I turned my head before my body, keeping an eye on the mirror. I stuck my leg out and tucked it back in, forcing my body to spin faster until everything was just a blur.

This time, I slowed my body gracefully and carefully, setting my foot down in the fifth position once more.

With an ounce of bravery, I forced myself to look at Madame Roussel. Her permanent frown was lightened, almost a smile. "That's good, good for today. Practice more."

"That's the biggest compliment you've ever given me," I said with a teasing grin.

She winked, an odd look for a woman with nonexistent smile lines. "You'll get more if you practice more. I'm locking up, scoot your booty, Karissia," she urged.

I picked up my bags and lightly chuckled at her pronunciation of my name.

Hastily, grabbing my sneakers and not bothering to take off my slippers, I "scooted my booty" into the winter air that stung my skin.

"Good night," she said as she slid into her car.

Snowflakes drifted from the sky as I sat on the freezing cement to change my shoes. The cold sidewalk felt unbelievably amazing on my worn-out muscles as I sat.

Each time I would complain to my mom about being sore, she'd ask if I was ready to quit. This baffled me. I was a ballet dancer with calloused feet to prove that my skill was earned through pain. Nothing in my life had brought me joy like dancing did. It was—

"Hey, Karissa," said a familiar masculine voice.

I shot my head up and felt my blood drain out of my face. "Lucas!" I practically shouted. "Hi!"

He pulled up his jeans and sat right by my side, so close his arm was brushing mine. "It's been a hot minute, yeah?"

I prayed with every ounce of energy that I wasn't visibly blushing. "Yeah, Earth Science B last year, right?"

He chuckled, making me swoon. Lucas was always a normally happy guy, with a crooked lopsided smile, but when he was genuinely happy, he had breathtaking dimples. I would do anything to see those dimples every day. "Dang, girl, you've got a good memory."

I let out an ugly laugh and instantly regretted it. "Well, that was the most entertaining class since Mrs. DeAnna's kindergarten class."

"Oh, man, I totally forgot about her!" he said loudly. "Do you remember back on that playground when you tried to eat a wood chip?"

I put my hand over his mouth impulsively. "Lucas! I was six years old!"

Your hand is on his lips! I screamed at myself inside my head. My heart pounded, and I dropped my hand back onto my lap. "Uh, so how's football going?"

Lucas laughed and looked at the ground. "It's not bad. Haven't seen your brother there in a while."

"Really?" I said, shocked. "How come? Aren't you still the quarterback?"

He seemed embarrassed by the recognition. "Yeah, I'm actually starting this year."

"Congratulations!"

"Ah, thanks," he said sheepishly. "But, yeah, I haven't seen Matt in ages! He used to be our starting wide receiver, but he hasn't come since open field back in June."

"Speak of the devil," I muttered as Matt's broken truck squealed into the parking lot. "Um, it was good to see you again, Lucas."

He stood and picked up my bag with my sweaty clothes. "Yeah, you too, Karissa! Maybe sometime I'll have to come watch you dance."

I accepted the bag and looked at my shoes. "That'd be cool."

"And you know, if you wanted, maybe we could do something afterward," he suggested casually.

"That'd be really fun," I said lamely.

He handed me a pen and held out his hand. "Write down your number and I'll call you."

I dropped the pen twice and messed up three numbers before my phone number was messily written on his palm. "Text me anytime," I said as I started walking toward Matt's truck.

He looked at me, dead serious. "No, I'll call you."

I squealed inside my head. "Sounds great. Bye, Lucas!" Without looking back, I jumped into my brother's car.

Matt shifted gears and sped across the icy parking lot.

"I thought Mom was picking me up," I asked, looking out the window at an ominous white van parked adjacent to the studio.

"She went to get groceries," he said, his eyes barely peeking out from under his baseball cap. "How was dance class?"

"Good."

"Was that Lucas Carter you were talking to?" he asked, glancing my way with a teasing look.

"Yeah, and he said you haven't been at football in months," I added, happily watching his teasing look fade into fear.

"I'm on defense now," he obviously lied.

"Okay," I said sarcastically. "Well, I can't wait to see a 135-pound kid play defense on varsity football."

"I am not 135 pounds," he shot back.

"And you're not playing football," I raised an eyebrow.

"Just shut up, and I won't tell Mom you were with Lucas Carter," he blackmailed.

I scoffed, watching him run through a stop sign nonchalantly. "What do I care if Mom knows I talked to Lucas?"

"Your funeral is gonna be a lot of fun."

He drifted into his spot under the broken basketball hoop and jumped out of the truck. I threw my bag over my shoulder and followed, almost tripping over the twin's bikes as I did.

The door hinges creaked as Matt shoved the door open. The smell of burnt spaghetti sauce greeted us, entrapping the kitchen heavily.

We heard a crash from the living room, followed by a loud howl. Matt let out a long string of curse words and went to check on the culprit of the noise.

I looked at my mom, standing in front of the stove where the smell originated. With one hand on the spoon and the other holding her phone to her ear, she waved with a pinkie and turned back to the burning dinner.

"How many times have you been told that this is a no-no?" Matt disciplined harshly. "You broke the lamp!"

I walked into the toy-invested living room and pulled the six-year-old from his tight grip. "Are you alright, Taylor?"

Her tears streamed endlessly down her rosy cheeks. "I saw if you pulled fast enough, nothing would fall."

I looked at the table runner on the carpet next to the shattered lamp. "You tried the tablecloth trick?" She nodded, guilt plastered over her bright green eyes. "Where's Tyler?"

"Playing with Brady." She continued to cry.

I looked up at Matt and motioned to the broken porch door. He grumbled more but walked out to find Tyler and the wheezy dog. "Now, Taylor, will you help me clean this up?"

"No!"

"Why?"

She looked at the glass lamp, in pieces embedded in the carpet. "It's dangerous, and I'm little."

"Go get me the vacuum, now."

Taylor made a sour face and stormed dramatically to the hall closet. A terrible sound screeched its way across the already scratched kitchen floor as she drug the vacuum by its wheels.

I cringed but didn't yell at her anymore as we began cleaning. Her lip quivered endlessly while we shoved the clay lamp into trash bags. My scolding voice rang in my ears, disciplining a toddler for using her imagination. "Taylor, guess what."

"What?" she asked shakily.

"I need new leggings for dance," I fibbed. "Would you like to come to buy some with me when I go?"

Her eyes instantly brightened. "Are you going to Discount Daily Dance?"

"Yes, ma'am." I tied the trash bag and set it by the sliding glass door. "Wanna come?"

"Are you kidding?" she cheered. "Heck yeah, I want to come! When?"

"I'm not sure, but I promise I won't go without you." I held out my pinkie.

She grinned, looping her pinkie through mine, and together, we kissed our thumbs. "You think I'll be able to dance like you one day?"

"Tay, you're almost better than me already," I teased. "Now I'm going to go shower before Mom calls me Krusty Karissa again."

She giggled and skipped outside to find our brothers.

The stairs were crispy with spilled milk and bubbles. I cringed with each step, wanting nothing more than to dial a carpet shampoo company that instant. The house creaked under my feet as I dodged backpacks, clothes, and dog toys before sliding into my room.

Or should I say, Matt and I's room.

One side, divided by a homemade blanket curtain, had an unmade twin bed, sweatshirts strung across a cluttered desk, and a heavy smell of sweat. The other side had a perfectly made bed, clothes folded neatly in a partially broken dresser, and a well-organized desk.

Unfortunately, mine was the former. By the time I went to school, work, then rehearsal, I barely had time to breathe, let alone clean the room. The project of the hoarders would have to wait another day.

Once again, the warm water was nonexistent from my nightly showers, which meant Mom hadn't gotten around to calling the repairman. Maybe the internet would be useful in fixing a water heater.

Goosebumps covered me like chicken pox while I made my way to the kitchen, shaking the freezing droplets from my hair.

Taylor and Tyler sat on the barstools, spaghetti sauce smeared on their chubby faces. They didn't so much as glance my way as I walked in, too busy tossing noodles to Brady, who had somehow gotten in the house.

I ignored the severely overweight dog and dished myself some lukewarm pasta. Matt dodged all three of us and slid out the door unnoticed by Mom, who was *still* on the phone.

"Kay, guess what!" Tyler practically shouted.

"Hm?" I responded, half listening.

"I get to be a wide receiver in football. I got my position today after school," he announced proudly, his lisp making him blow spaghetti sauce across the counter.

I couldn't help but smile. He was still sporting his T-shirt and cleats. "That is so cool, dude."

"They made an exception for him because he's so good!" Taylor informed me. "You're not supposed to play mitey-mite football till you're seven."

I held a finger to my lips. "I know that, but Mom doesn't, so be quiet."

She nodded aggressively. "Matt signed the forms."

"What forms?" my mom asked as she hung up the phone.

I fumbled for a response. Matt was much better at the excuses, the improv lying. "Um, for Taylor's lessons at dance. You signed them yesterday." It wasn't subtle, but at least it was true.

She looked between the three of us. "Right," she said, drawing out the words. "So, sweetie, how was dance today?"

I shrugged. "It was fine, I finally mastered the—"

Her phone woke and erupted into chiming her three-note ringtone. She held up a finger and answered it without hesitation.

I took a breath and stabbed my stale bread aggressively, hoping it would help me bite my tongue.

Tyler tugged on my T-shirt. "What did you master today, Kay?"

I let myself smile at the twins, still hanging on my every word. "I mastered ten spins in a row while starting and ending in the fifth position."

Tyler tossed another piece of bread to Brady. "I didn't understand one word of that."

Taylor slurped an undercooked noodle. "I wish I did! But I'm proud of Karissa, I think."

I chuckled.

My mom slid her phone back into her scrubs and rubbed her eyes. "Sorry, honey. What were you saying?"

"Dance was fine," I muttered.

"Great, so quick question."

Oh no, here it comes.

"Could you babysit tomorrow night?" she asked, pleading in her eyes.

I stifled a groan. "Mom, for real? I don't know. I have to work tomorrow, and the deadline for October scholarships is in a week. Why can't Matt just do it?"

"He has football practice tomorrow," her voice was getting tight, and her eyes focused on me.

"I can't take work off, Mom."

"He can't miss football if he wants to get scholarships," she raised an eyebrow, challenging me to see how far I would push it.

"He can miss *one* practice. I need to work to pay for college," I said stubbornly.

Though she wasn't very good at listening to my day, she was always good at hearing the other side of an argument. "Fine, he can babysit if you do the dishes tonight," she said, resisting a smile.

"Deal!" I shook her hand and jumped up. Without another thought, I threw the dirty plates and cups into the leaky dishwasher. Though I'm pretty sure neither of the twins ate a single bite of their food.

Brady's full-stomach groan made me think he agreed.

While Mom paid our well-overdue bills, I took Taylor and Tyler and threw their sauce-covered faces into the tub.

The smell of their strawberry bubbles floated around me, making my heart rate ease. Though the twins swore they were old enough to bathe on their own, they had overflowed the tub twice. So instead of spending all night mopping up inches of cold bathwater, I sat on the floor and supervised.

Tyler dumped an incredible amount of shampoo on his spiky hair and began scrubbing. "Karissa?"

"Yes, QB?" I said, looking up from the four-hundred-page calculus book.

He ignored the nickname and lowered his voice. "Do you think Daddy has a girlfriend?"

I dropped the textbook, making the house shudder in response. "What in the world makes you think that?"

Taylor shot her eyes up from the rubber duck she was currently waterboarding with a dishtowel. "Ty! We do not speak of that man."

Closing the book, I knelt by the bathtub. "Tyler, I don't know what Dad is doing, but I don't like to think about it because there's not really a point. He made his decision, and we have to make ours. Are we going to stay and be a part of the Anderson family, or are we going to be grumpy and mean?"

"Like Matt?" Taylor chirped.

I tried to think of something that wouldn't sound like I agreed with her. "Matt is in high school, and high school makes you tired and stressed and sometimes mean. But that doesn't mean we can be mad at Matt for being overwhelmed, okay?"

"He could lighten up, that's all I'm saying," she said with a sassy voice.

I clapped my hands together, making them both jump. "Alright, start drying off, it's bedtime."

They groaned and grumbled, but the limited warm water supply ran out, and it was time for pajamas.

Taylor sat on the edge of her bed, wrapped in a yellow towel, instructing me which pajamas would be perfect. Tyler lay in his spaceship bed, telling her to "wrap it up before morning was here." Finally, unicorns won, and Taylor scrambled into her polka dot comforter.

The door slammed downstairs, and indistinct yelling began almost immediately. Wonderful, Matt was home right as everything was finished.

Taylor sat up, a saddened look on her face. "What are they saying?"

I clicked on their butterfly night-light and ignored the question. "Fan on or off?"

"On!" they yelled together.

"Kay, did Dad ever play with us?" Tyler asked.

I walked to his side and smoothed down his wild hair. "Go to bed, kid. Questions like this will keep you up all night long if you let them. And the starting wide receiver needs his sleep."

"Yeah, he does," he mumbled into his pillow.

"Good night," I said, turning off the light and shutting the door.

Yes, the twins were hyper, crazy, imaginative, and endlessly loud, but how could you not love them? They were kids with huge, beautiful personalities.

"Every single night you do this! Do not call it a one-time thing!" Mom screamed from downstairs.

"It's not like you even notice me when I am here! Why do you care if I leave? You didn't when Dad did," Matt retorted.

"Too far," I whispered to myself, shutting myself into the room. The vents shook while the yelling continued for over two hours. Two hours where chemistry wasn't the most annoying thing in the house.

The sounds of Beethoven were rudely interrupted as a car alarm echoed through the thin walls. I whisked my headphones out of my ears and scampered to the window.

Sitting in front of the Green's driveway was another white van. Its left taillight shattered, thus the alarm. The man in the driver's seat got out and kicked the tire, swearing angrily. He took his time getting his keys out of his pocket and turning the alarm off.

"Rough night all around," I said to no one as I slid the curtains shut and began crawling into bed.

Just as I began dozing off, Matt stormed in and flipped the lights on, with no regard for the thought I might be asleep.

"Are you serious?" I whisper-yelled. "You've got to be joking, Matthew."

"Chill," was all he said, his voice filled with ice. He slid into bed, kicking his shoes off and starting to scroll on his phone.

I propped myself up on my elbow. "Turn off the light. You don't need it to look at your phone."

"You do it, you're the one who wants it off," he scoffed, turning his volume up even more.

Now I was wide awake, wanting to strangle him. "Matt! Turn it off. You're literally like three feet away."

He turned his back on me and ignored me.

I threw my pillow at the back of his head.

"Kay, stop it," he growled, throwing the pillow directly into my stomach.

Swallowing my anger and pride, I got up and flipped the lights off. Thanks to him, I had to stumble around the desks and dressers to find my bed.

"Yo! I still need to find my charger, turn it back on!"

"Argh!"

CHAPTER 2

"No problem, Susan," my mom said into her phone, her fake cheerfulness seeping into the speakers.

I slumped over my cereal, feeling half-dead.

Taylor and Tyler were the opposite as usual. They squealed and giggled, their mismatched outfits already wrinkled.

"You get over that stomach bug, you hear me?" Mom continued, adding a phony laugh. "Alright, buh-bye." She slid the phone across the counter and rubbed her eyes.

"Taking another shift?" I asked, dumping the rest of my breakfast down the sink.

"Susan seems to have the flu," she said as if she was trying to convince herself it was true. "I'll be home when you get up tomorrow, alright?"

Matt walked past the kitchen, snatching a banana off the rack. "Leaving now."

"Matthew!" Mom called as he started out the front door.

He stopped, shoving his hands into his pockets and giving her a nasty look. "What?"

"You told me you could take the twins to school," she said slowly like he was stupid.

"Mom, that's ten minutes out of the way!" he yelled.

I picked up the twin's backpacks and started out to the truck. They followed, knowing the drill every single morning.

"You know, if Matt would just say 'okay,' we would get to school on time," Taylor informed me and Tyler.

"Or if Mom reminded him at night, he'd get up earlier," Tyler added.

"Get in the car seats and buckle up," I said absentmindedly. My focus was stuck on the van with the broken taillight, still parked in front of the Green's house. Its driver was wearing aviator sunglasses despite the sun just barely peeking out over the city.

Matt slammed the front door, announcing to the world he was furious. "Get in, now," he instructed as he started the truck.

I glanced back at the van once more before climbing into the passenger seat. "Did the Greens get a new car?"

"What?" he shot back, not bothering to check for cars as he peeled onto the highway.

"That van has been parked there all night," I said quietly.

"And?"

"Never mind," I grumbled, leaning my head on the window.

He grabbed my arm and pulled me up. "Get your forehead grease off my window."

I raised an eyebrow, challenging him. "Excuse me?"

He didn't respond, knowing he had directed his anger too harshly.

The parent aid angrily blew her whistle as Matt cut off an entire line of buses at the elementary. He stopped in front of the school and looked back at the twins. "Get out, y'all," he instructed.

"*Y'all?*" I snorted.

"Don't start with me," he shot back.

The twins eagerly jumped out of the truck and waved until we were out of sight. "Tyler reminds me a lot of Dad," I said quietly.

"Great, another tramp in the family."

"Matt!" I almost yelled.

He smiled, almost darkly. "There's a lot worse I could say about him, Kay."

"I'm just saying. Tyler is always questioning everything, he's proud, he's funny." I thought back on my life. "Can't you see it?"

Matt clenched his jaw and parked in his usual spot. "You bring up Dad one more time today, you're sleeping in the garage."

"Like you have that kind of authority." I crawled out of the truck and stormed off. All I wanted was to have a fun conversation about our brother, but he couldn't be mature about that.

The first bell rang, making this day just that much better. I tightened my backpack straps and took off.

The sound of teenagers rushing to their first hour filled the hallway. The utter chaos and stereotypes of it all made it seem like a badly written movie. Two friends shoved their buddy into a locker. A couple made out on the locker next to it. A group of girls huddled together, gossiping while texting simultaneously. A robotic car swerved under my muddy shoes, making me stumble. A football flew over my head, and, of course, Jonathan Sloan, Lucas's best friend, caught it in his left hand.

"Yo, did you see that?" he asked no one in particular.

"We saw," I said, smiling as I passed. "May that stroke your ego in the best way possible."

"Karissa, charming as always." He winked, making not sure whether he was mocking or flirting.

"You know me." I shrugged.

He caught up to me as I continued to walk. "Have you seen Matt lately?"

I half scoffed, wondering if he was being serious. "Well, you know he's my twin, and we share a room and truck, right?"

"Duh." He flipped the ball around in his ginormous palms. "I mean like the fact that he hasn't been to practice in ages. Coach is playing Montgomery, and he *sucks*. We need him back before the big game."

I looked back at my brother, his baseball cap covering half his face as per usual. "You should tell him that, it'd mean a lot." I motioned toward him.

Jonathan spotted him closing the red locker and lightly punched my shoulder. "You're the bomb, Anderson. See you around. Say hi to Lucas for me, okay?"

My cheeks flushed red. Had Lucas been talking about me? What did Jonathan mean by that, and how could I find out?

Jonathan clapped Matt's shoulder, making him jump. Matt would be furious if he found out how I had meddled. But I didn't have time for that. I had a chemistry quiz.

Once a year, since I could remember, our teachers would get us in a meeting and ask us about our futures. Each time they'd ask "What do you want to be when you grow up?" my answer would be the same every time, "A dancer." They would look at me with their passive-aggressive smiles and say, "Oh, that's great. Now, what's the practical plan?"

Even today, my answer remains "dancer," so tell me why I need to learn the functions of a smooth endoplasmic reticulum.

"Hey!" shouted a voice as I left my first hour.

I looked up and saw Amber, the one girl I could call a true friend. Amber was the girl who would always ask if I wanted to hang out even after my dad left. Those long weeks when none of us left the house, she would show up with old movies and enough junk food to feed an army. Though we both had gotten busy and would rarely hang out outside of school, she never stopped putting effort in.

"Hi!"

"Dude, you've been MIA for like three weeks now. What's up?" she asked, her red curls bouncing like sparks off a fire.

I laughed. "It's been crazy. I have school, rehearsal, and work almost every day. What about you? What's new?"

She half shrugged, making her backpack slip off her shoulder. "Honestly, nothing. My mom's been hinting at having *another* baby." She groaned. "I swear if she gets even a little serious about it, I'll move out."

I gasped and snorted. "Are you kidding? Your house will pop if you bring one more kid in."

"Last week, I almost slapped my dad in the grocery store," she continued, not caring how loud she was talking. "He stopped in front of the newborn diapers and got all melancholy."

"I can't even remember all of your siblings," I admitted.

She held up her hands, counting as she named them. "Kambryn, Colby, Kalise, Joshua, Brad, Avery, Taten, Macy, Jackson, and Morgan. Though that doesn't seem right…am I missing someone?"

"I can't handle the twins. I can't even imagine nine kids!" Her family baffled me. "Wait, what's going on with you and Daniel?"

Amber blew a stream of air out. "Oh, you know high school. 'I saw Daniel with Katie yesterday.' Well, they're both in debate, so I sure hope you did!" she said quickly, half of what she said not making any sense.

"Karissa!" someone shouted from behind me.

I whipped around, afraid to look as I recognized the voice.

Lucas was sprinting down the hall, precisely dodging between the hundreds of students in his way.

Amber and I stood awkwardly, just watching as the sea of students swam around us.

Finally, he caught up to us and slid directly in front of me. "Hi, how's it going?" he asked breathlessly. "How are you, Amber?"

"Doing swell, Carter," she said, giving me a teasing smile. "If you guys would excuse me, I've gotta run to Nutrition." She kicked the back of my knees and almost ran off.

"Um, so anyway," Lucas continued, his words running faster than he did. "I was going to call you yesterday, but I shattered my phone. Like legitimately," he rambled. "Which may sound like a sad excuse, so I brought evidence." He held up his phone in a ziplock bag, which was quite literally shattered to pieces. "Anyway, since I don't have this anymore. How does lunch today sound? I know your schedule after school is crazy, so I thought we could do this today and then go out sometime this weekend for a real date."

I laughed in disbelief. "That's perfect! Um, where do you want to meet?"

"Front of the school?"

I just nodded lamely until the awkwardness was suffocating. "See you then, Lucas."

*****

"So wait," I said in between giggles, "how did it shatter?"

The sun was beaming on our faces as we sat on the tables in the schoolyard. An empty pizza box sat at our feet, and we leaned back, satisfied with full stomachs.

Lucas laughed with me, his loose curls moving with him. "So I'm running late last night, right?"

I didn't know if it was a rhetorical or real question, so I just shrugged, my smile never fading.

"My mom was hosting a craft night or whatever at the school gym. So after seeing you at the studio, I was trying to hurry, or she'd be mad. I threw my bag in the car and peeled out. Soon after, I was at a red light and decided to plug my phone in to listen to music. And that's when I figured I left my phone in the studio's parking lot," he explained, using his hands to illustrate every detail.

Wow, he's the best storyteller, I thought as he gave me his crooked grin.

"I pulled into the lot and started searching, pretty mad that I had lost it. Honestly, Karissa, I looked *everywhere*," he said, pretending to be frustrated.

"It's not that big of a parking lot," I teased.

He scoffed and nudged my shoulder. "Oh, hush, Anderson. It was very dark."

"Alright, whatever, go on," I egged him on.

"So I was getting back in my car, convinced I had left it at home or something, and slammed the door shut as hard as I could," he said slowly.

It took me a few seconds to register that the story was over. "O-oh my goodness! That is awful!"

"But, hey, at least it wasn't my leg or finger," he said happily.

I picked up the ziplock bag of phone pieces. "That's the saddest thing I've heard in a while."

"Yeah, I live a depressing life," he said sarcastically, shaking his shoulders goofily. "Hey, you're really pretty, Karissa."

My cheeks were on fire. I couldn't handle myself. I stared at the hole in my shoe until the blush died down. "Thank you."

The bell rang, interrupting the moment of contentment.

"Shall we?" he held out his hand and bowed.

"For the star quarterback of a high school, you are a full dork," I said, accepting his hand and trying not to panic.

He laughed so hard his face went pink. I even got to see those rare, beautiful dimples.

"Well, I s—" My foot caught on the edge of the seat as I tried to get off the table. Lucas tried to grab my arm, but it was too late. I went from completely vertical to slamming my face on the concrete in less than a second.

Ouch

"Oh my gosh! Are you okay?" he yelled.

I couldn't breathe. I was worried if I sat up too quickly, my brain would spill onto the ground. Warm blood seeped down my temple and into my hair. "Oh geez, that was embarrassing," I mumbled.

Hands wrapped under my armpits and lifted me up and onto the table. "That was a serious fall, dude. Are you alright?"

I smiled at how close he was to my face. "Hi," I whispered.

His eyebrows raised in full concern. He knelt in front of me. "Karissa, are you going to live?"

"Thanks, yeah, I'm fine," I grinned and then winced.

"I'm going to go get a teacher or something," Lucas said awkwardly.

Without thinking, I yanked his arm back before he could walk away. "Lucas, I'm fine! A little blood never hurt anybody." I couldn't believe I had said that.

"Karissa, I hate to break it to you, but you have blood dripping down your chin," he said, his voice so serious it surprised me.

I half shrugged, not quite sure what I was supposed to say.

"Man, should I take you to the hospital?" he asked himself as he moved my hair away from my face.

I got a whiff of his cologne and felt my legs shake. "I'm fine, okay? We're gonna be late."

"I thought dancers weren't supposed to be clumsy," he said, carefully helping me to my feet. "Come on, let's at least find a paper towel to wipe that blood off."

I didn't argue as he led me into the school, his hand placed firmly on my back. "I guess that's what makes me a unique dancer."

Lucas pushed past the raging teenagers and shoved me into the nearest girl's bathroom.

Katie Landon stood over the sink, applying fresh blush to the thick foundation that coated her face. She smirked as Lucas and I walked in together. "Well, well, I heard the rumors, but I never thought Swan Lake would do something so scandalous."

Lucas's hand trembled on my back. "Out."

Katie winked. "You got it, have fun," she said with a flirtatious wave.

"Ah, high school," I said in a singsongy voice. "Gotta love it."

He laughed and looked at the closed door. "To be fair, we did just run into the girl's bathroom like hormone-filled teenagers."

"Har-har." I laughed, hoping I wasn't blushing.

"Alright, hop on the counter," Lucas instructed casually.

I blinked, making my head pound. "What did we just finish talking about, Mr. Carter?"

Blood rushed to *his* cheeks, and he shook his head furiously. "No, no, no! You're hurt, I'm gonna help."

My chest lit on fire, watching him get nervous and embarrassed, but now it was my turn to be embarrassed. "I'm not getting on the counter, Lucas."

He raised an eyebrow, fighting a contagious grin. "Karissa, now."

I folded my arms, much like Taylor did when she was pouting.

"Fine." He shrugged, making me think I had won. Suddenly, his hands were around my thighs, and I was in the air. He lifted me onto the counter and turned away.

I stared at the ground, unable to move. My heart was pounding like a sledgehammer. *Did that really just happen?* I asked myself, even the voice in my head was in disbelief.

Lucas wetted a paper towel and began wiping off the blood.

I closed my eyes, unable to stand the intense stinging.

My pain must have been displayed clearly on my face. "You remember when we did the musical in fifth grade? You could dance like a professional Broadway star, but you sang like a wounded bird." He laughed, grabbing two more paper towels.

"Oh yeah? Like you were so great!" I teased as I poked his shoulder. "You walked out, threw up, and ran backstage!"

His neck turned bright red. "I thought we agreed to never talk about that again, Karissa."

I laughed.

He swore under his breath. "This looks really bad," he admitted. My hand rose to touch it, but he caught it. "You better just look." His voice was serious.

I cautiously turned to look at the mirror. My temple was open, a legit gash stretched into my skin. "My mom's a nurse. I'll just pop by the hospital," I said, trying to stay calm and laugh it off.

Lucas stepped back. "Oh, Karissa, I am *so* sorry," he said, rubbing the back of his head. "I feel so bad!"

"Hey, dude, for real, it's not your fault," I said, hopping off the counter. "Please don't feel bad. I can be the worst klutz."

"I'm so sorry," he said over and over. "I promise I'll make it up to you. I swear."

CHAPTER 3

"If my boss finds us and I get fired, I blame you," my mom scolded. My legs were freezing as I sat on the floor of the supply closet, a needle going in and out of my head.

"I cannot believe you sometimes, Karissa," she sighed "Do you know how much this would cost if I couldn't do this for you? Do you know how many patients need me right now? Do you know how late I'm going to have to stay now?"

"I'm sorry," I whined. "It's not like I meant to face plant onto solid concrete."

"No, but you're a dancer, you're supposed to be graceful," my mom continued, not wanting to admit it was a mistake. "I have paid for dance classes since you were two years old, and this is what I get for it."

I rolled my eyes but didn't respond, knowing it wouldn't matter what I said.

Matt grumbled in the corner, only agreeing to drive me when Mom promised to excuse him for the rest of the day. "How long is this going to take?"

"Shut your mouth, Matt," our mom snapped. "Do you need to call into work and tell them what happened, Kay?"

I resisted the urge to shake my head. "It'll be fine."

My mom finished stitching up my temple and kissed the top of my head. "Mwah."

Oh, good, she wasn't really angry. I looked up at her and smiled. "Thanks, Mom."

She cupped my face with her hands. "Hey, you need to be more careful. I made that head, so take good care of it. You hear?"

I nodded. "You got it. Come on, Matt."

My mom held up a finger. "Wait, let me talk to Matt for a second. Go to the lobby and wait, *patiently*."

"Mom—"

"Take my car to work," she said, her face serious.

"Okay," I whispered to myself as I snagged her keys.

*****

"Joanna's Diner, if you're not rocking, we're not rocking. Would you like to try our new bopping hopping jalapeno poppers?" I answered the phone. They hung up.

My apron was already stained with thick milkshake cream. My hair was standing up around my hat. But at least the tip jar was overflowing.

"Karissa, my main dude," my boss Tony said as I set the phone back into its cradle. "How have you been?"

I looked around at my coworkers slowly moving, our restaurant as empty as a beehive in the winter. "Um, good."

"How's your family?" he asked.

"They're always up to something." I laughed awkwardly. "Tyler's starting receiver on his team, and Taylor is in beginner ballet."

He itched his salt-and-pepper goatee and gave his room-filling laugh. "Those two are always up to something." His face became serious. "How's Matthew?"

"I'm not sure. He's really quiet and always angry about something," I said hesitantly. "We used to be inseparable, now we can't find things to talk about."

"Yeah, I'm sure. He and your father were quite close, weren't they?" he asked, his voice solemn.

"Very."

He looked around the empty restaurant. "You know what? I can help clean up tonight. Go home. Spend time with your family," he said with an overjoyed smile.

"Are you sure?" I asked, feeling awkward. "I mean Mindy and the baby are probably anxious to see you."

He shrugged it off. "I'm not super excited to go change diapers, so yeah. Get out of here, kid."

Ecstatic that I didn't have to stay another three hours doing nothing, I thanked him repeatedly and ran out.

I looked up at the snowflakes gently falling from the foggy gray clouds. As they caught my eyelashes, they reminded me of ash falling from a fire.

My phone rang, making me jump. I squinted at the unrecognized number and held it up to my ear. "Hello?"

"You're alive! It's a religious miracle!" Lucas yelled from the other end.

I giggled. "Hey, Lucas, how's it going?"

"Well, you know I was actually calling to ask you that," he said with his beautiful laugh.

"I'm doing fantastic."

"Is that sarcasm I'm sensing?"

I dramatically gasped. "Me? Sarcastic? Oh, never."

He laughed again. "Alright, I'll take your word for it. Anyway, I got a flip phone today, classy I know, so consider this my number."

"Oh, a flip phone! I'm so jealous," I said, this time without an ounce of sarcasm.

He chuckled. "You know, surprisingly, I am actually pumped. Not having the obligation of a smartphone is gonna be awesome."

"Have you named the phone yet?"

"Rex," he said sheepishly.

I stopped in my tracks to laugh out loud. "That is adorable."

"Oh, why thank you, Swan Lake," he said, laughing with me. "In all seriousness, can I pick you up from your studio at seven tomorrow for a movie?"

"Absolutely," I said with a smile in my voice.

"Awesome! See you then, Karissa," he said as he hung up the phone.

I shut off my phone and practically floated all the way home.

The door groaned as I walked into the kitchen, my feet sticking on the messy hardwood floor.

"Where have you been?" Matt demanded from the living room.

I frowned at him for ruining my good mood. "Work, you knew that."

"I had football practice, and you made me miss it," he grumped.

The house was way too quiet. I narrowed my eyes at him. "Yeah, freaking right, Matt. You did not. Where are the twins?"

"What do you mean, I was not at practice? I can't miss it. I need college scholarships!"

I half ignored him. "And I need to pay for college. Where are the twins?" I asked again.

"They're playing in their room."

"Quietly?"

We both shared a look and took off, running up the stairs. Our feet slid dramatically as we stopped short in their room.

There they were, the little devils. They sat on the ground, innocently giggling while piles of hair sat around them, scissors in both of their hands.

Matt let out a long string of curses before beginning to yell at them. "Are you serious?"

"What?" Tyler whined. "You told us to play upstairs, and so we are!" he argued.

"I am so dead," Matt said, putting his head in his hands.

My mouth hung open in complete and utter shock. Taylor's hair was uneven and so short it barely touched her chin. Tyler's hair was close to a buzz cut.

I looked at Matt, his fear written plainly on his face. "Okay, um, I can probably get it even. Then we tell Mom they got gum in their hair and we couldn't get it out," I suggested.

"Mom will never believe it!" Matt screamed.

"You got a better idea?" I asked, just as loudly.

He gritted his teeth and balled up his fists. "Fine."

I set up chairs in the bathroom and wrapped towels around their shoulders. "Okay, this is gonna be fine. It's gonna be easy." Carefully, I lifted the eyebrow-trimming scissors and began cutting.

By the time I was done, at least Tyler's hair was straight, and Taylor's was more than a mangled bob.

They giggled at each other while Matt swept up the hair.

Downstairs, the garage door opened. My heart stopped. Matt was right, Mom was going to kill us.

"Matt? Tay? Tyler? Where are you guys?" she called.

"We're upstairs, Mommy!" Taylor yelled back.

"And we have a surprise!" Tyler screeched.

Matt glared daggers at him.

I could hear my heart pounding in my ears.

She walked upstairs and gasped as she saw her kids. Her hand slowly covered her mouth. "What happened?" she said through gritted teeth. Her face was growing redder by the second.

Taylor stuck out her hip and flipped her short hair. "Ta-da!"

Matt looked like he was going to faint at any second.

"I got home, and Matt was in the twin's room," I said, jumping in to save him. "They got into our gum and got it stuck in their hair. I helped him calm them down, but we couldn't get it out. So we had to cut it."

Mom looked like she was ready to cry, scream, or both. "Why didn't you try scrubbing it out o-or peanut butter or something?" she croaked.

"We did!" Matt squeaked. "It wouldn't come out!"

She sighed, ready to give up. "Matt, Karissa, go downstairs. I'll bathe the twins and deal with you in a second."

Matt and I shared a guilty look and solemnly walked down the stairs.

We sat at the kitchen table and awaited our doom.

"Why aren't you playing football?" I asked, my voice barely above a whisper.

He scoffed and stared at a grape juice stain on the ground.

"Come on," I urged. "Didn't Johnathan talk to—"

Matt angrily shoved his chair back. "I knew it! I knew it!" he screamed. "You meddled in my life, just like always."

I swore in my head. "Johnathan was asking if you were going to play the next game. I didn't know, so I just told him to ask you, alright?"

"No, not alright!" he yelled back. "Ever since Dad left, you've had a mission to keep everything normal. Well, guess what, Karissa, it's not. In case you haven't noticed, it's awful. Mom doesn't give a crap about us unless we do something wrong. Case in point? Did she ask you about how your head is? Did she ask you about work? No, she just saw an opportunity to yell at us and took it."

My breath caught in my throat as he continued. "Matt, I—"

"Shut up, Karissa, and just get out of my life!" His words echoed off the walls.

Mom cleared her throat behind us.

We whipped around, knowing without a shadow of a doubt that she had heard the whole thing.

"First off," she said quietly. "Matthew, I asked you to watch them for two hours, and you couldn't even do that."

Matt was still filled with the energy of his anger and shook his head.

She turned to me as I struggled to keep my emotions off my face. "Karissa, your first resort was to cut their hair? You could have at least waited for me to come home and let me do it."

"I'm sorry," I whispered pathetically.

"Moving on to what I just heard," she said, her voice strained. "Matt, are you going to football practice at all?"

He turned his glare away from the floor and onto me.

"Don't look at your sister," Mom commanded. "Look at me and answer."

"I am, I just had to miss today because *you* told me to miss," he said, making his voice as innocent as possible."

She wanted to argue, she wanted to get a full confession out of him, but she was drained. "You're grounded for two weeks. You will go to school, practice, and come right home. If I catch you sneaking out again, I'll take away your phone for a month."

He wanted to say something but was smart enough not to.

Now it was my turn. "Karissa, you are grounded for the rest of the week. You will go to dance, work, and come straight home."

I jumped out of my chair, tired of being pushed around all night. "Why am I grounded? All I did was try to help Matt."

"You cut off my babies' hair. You should have called me."

I felt like crying. "Mom, how do you not see how unfair this is?"

Her eyebrows were arched, ready to launch into full beast mode at any second. "Do not push me."

"I have a date tomorrow!" I blurted out.

Her mouth twitched in a smile. "Who?"

"Lucas kinda asked me out," I said, blushing and looking away.

She let herself relax. "Ah, finally."

I blinked in surprise. "Finally?"

"You guys have been in love since the third grade!" Mom smiled more. "But fine. You may go out tomorrow if you promise to babysit Saturday night."

"Deal," I said, relaxing myself.

She pulled me and my brother into a tight hug and kissed our cheeks. "You guys know I love you, and I'm so proud of both of you."

My brother glared at me in the midst of our hug.

CHAPTER 4

"Good, now let's do it with the music," Madame Roussel instructed.

I nodded and took a deep breath. My feet were throbbing with intense pain. I was sweaty and dehydrated, but inside, I was pumped.

The piano intro started, cueing me to fly across the studio. I closed my eyes and twirled, the music controlling me. My clumsiness disappeared as if it had never existed. I gracefully leaped and spun dramatically across the smooth floor.

Here was the killer move. I put my feet in the fifth position and spun myself around, faster and faster. The world turned into a blur as I perfected the spin.

When I finished, I leaped to the other side of the room and did the final pose, pretending I wasn't as out of breath as I was.

I heard clapping in the corner of the room and whipped my head around. Lucas was sitting on the bench in the back, clapping and grinning like a chimp. The color drained out of my face. I clenched my teeth and fought back my smile.

Madame Roussel looked amused at my embarrassment. "I was going to tell you that your boyfriend was here, but you were doing so good I didn't want to stop you."

"Oh, he's not, I mean, he's my...uh—" I stammered.

"I'm her date for the evening." He smirked, saving the day once again.

This time, I let the smile take over my face. "I'll go get changed, super quick."

Madame Roussel patted my shoulder stiffly. "Very good, Karissa. Keep practicing."

"Thanks." I didn't dare look at Lucas as I went to the dressing room and quickly changed into my favorite outfit. "Come on, Karissa," I said to the panicked girl in the mirror. "He's just a person, you have no reason to let your heart beat like a jackhammer."

She was never convinced.

But I was ready, and it was time. I shook out my hair one last time before sauntering out of the studio. My heart thudded as I saw Lucas's navy blue truck waiting beside the van with the broken taillight.

He jumped out of the truck and rushed to the passenger door. The loud heater greeted me as I thanked him and slid into the seat.

I stared out at the van, its tinted windows, and heavy doors.

"Karissa?"

It took me a minute to realize he had said something, and I didn't listen. "Sorry, what?"

"You alright?" he asked, throwing in a casual laugh.

I shook away my embarrassment. "Yeah, sorry, I've just...um what'd you say?"

He laughed again, making me want to melt right then and there. "I was gonna ask what I owed you for the stitches in your skull."

My goofy laugh flew out of my mouth before I could stop it. "Oh, this?"

A kiss would do fine, the persistent voice in my head suggested.

"Please don't worry about it, honestly." I waved my hand off. "My mom did it, so it didn't cost anything."

"How is your mom doing?"

I turned, shocked that he would care. "She's alright. She works a lot, which I get. Our house is a chaotic mess, so I'm sure the hospital is a break," I said, spilling way more than I wanted to.

"That's rough. Is Matt doing alright? It's been a hot minute since I've seen him," he said, flipping on his blinker.

I squinted, trying to think of how to describe him. "He's a teenager, that's for sure."

Lucas slid into a parking stall and smiled at the steering wheel. "Alright, shall we?"

I just nodded and popped the door open.

"Woah, woah, woah!" he said suddenly, making me jump. "Close that door, right now!"

My brow furrowed as I slowly shut the door again. He jumped out of his seat and sprinted to my side. "What kind of a gentleman would I be if I didn't open your doors?"

Weirdly enough, I felt like crying. "Yeah, come on, dude, catch up," I teased, not sure how else to thank him.

We walked side by side, our fingers brushing against each other as he led me into the theater. The heavenly smell of popcorn welcomed us as soon as he opened the door. I couldn't remember the last time I had been to a movie theater.

"Alright, what do you want to see?" he asked, putting his hand on my back.

I tried to fix my posture as he did. My eyes scanned over our options. There was a chick flick that would probably be the ideal date movie, but I had wanted to see the action movie when it came out a few weeks ago. I shrugged nonchalantly. "It's up to you."

He reached forward and tucked a loose piece of hair behind my ear. "Come on, I know you. You can't go anywhere and not have an opinion. Just say it, Karissa."

I laughed. "You got me," I said, pointing to the action movie.

Luckily, he laughed with me. "Thank goodness. I wanted to see that one too." He paid for the tickets and popcorn before guiding me to our auditorium.

The previews for a new musical were just starting. I pulled my phone out of my pocket and silenced it.

"Can I tell you a secret?" He leaned over and whispered in my ear.

I felt goosebumps rise up my neck but casually nodded. "Yeah," I whispered back.

It took him a few moments to stop smiling. "In the fourth grade, I was the one that dumped your water bottle in your backpack."

Trying to suppress my giggles, I faked a gasp. "Lucas Carter, how dare you."

He opened and closed his mouth. "I thought that if I tormented you enough, you would know I had a crush on you."

My heart skipped an entire beat. "I thought if I tagged you enough in flag football, you would know *I* had a crush on *you*."

We both smiled helplessly, inches apart.

Lucas was the one to break eye contact first. He looked down. "Hey, my mom will kill me if we don't take a picture. She's pumped I asked you out."

"Lucas, if you want a picture, just ask," I teased, bumping his shoulder. I handed him my phone, knowing his flip phone wouldn't be sufficient for a proper selfie.

He laughed with me and held up the phone for a selfie. I leaned next to his warm cheek, feeling his rough peach fuzz tickling my face, and smiled. He took a picture, the flash almost blinding us.

I relaxed, but he didn't move.

He turned, quicker than I thought possible, and kissed my cheek, his thumb snapping the picture.

That just happened! Lucas Carter just kissed your cheek! I screamed inside my head.

The lights dimmed.

The movie was hypnotizing, both of us were so absorbed in its plot that we barely acknowledged each other. Halfway through the movie, when the car chase scene was in its twelfth minute, I reached for the popcorn. Instantly, I felt something that made me want to vomit with pure adrenaline. Lucas's hand was touching mine.

I took a long breath, reminding myself of the pep talk I was given. With an insane amount of bravery, I set down the bowl and encased his fingers between my own. He rubbed his thumb over my knuckles, making my toes tingle with happiness.

My chest screamed in joy as I reminded myself I was on a date with Lucas Carter, *the* Lucas Carter. My gaze drifted toward him, his sharp jawline, his blue-green eyes, his dusty-blond hair, his overjoyed smile. He was effortlessly handsome. I couldn't pull my gaze away.

He caught my eye and broke into a grin. Tucking a hair behind my ear, he put a hand on my cheek. "You're…"

"You'll never take me alive," the movie screamed.

"So…"

"You're coming with me, intact or in pieces!"

"Beautiful…"

"We've got three seconds before the bomb goes off!"

"Karissa," he whispered.

I leaned in close, feeling as if gravity was pulling me like a magnet. He closed his eyes. I held my breath. My hand was on his chest. His fingers were in my hair. We were a moment apart.

The lights flickered on.

"You've got to be kidding me," Lucas said under his breath.

I couldn't help but laugh to shake away what had almost happened. "Oh, come on, Lucas," I said, standing up. "Don't make it *that* obvious."

He itched the back of his neck and grabbed my hand again. "I am not being obvious."

"Okay," I said sarcastically.

He led me out of the auditorium and back into the lobby. The theater was packed with people waiting for the next showing of the movie we had just seen.

"Carter, my man!" Jonathan called from across the room.

Lucas smiled at me, and we made our way to see his friend. "What's up?"

To my surprise, Amber was leaning against Jonathan's shoulder. She gave me the same shocked look.

"I guess I can't be mad about *you* not telling *me* you had a date!" she said, jokingly poking my shoulder.

I punched her back and laughed. "You player." I grinned with a wink.

"We've been in the talking stage for *so* long, and he finally asked me out yesterday," she said with a big grin.

"Yay!" I said loud enough for all of Chicago to hear. "I expect a long text from you tonight, got it?"

"Only if you send me one first!" she said excitedly. "Is this your first date?"

I nodded, not wanting to explain the first date where I had quite literally almost died of embarrassment.

She smiled genuinely. "I'm so happy for you, Kay. This is incredible. You needed a win tonight."

"I'm sorry?" I asked, wondering which aspect of my life she could be referring to.

Her face changed. "Oh."

My shoulders tensed, grabbing Lucas's attention. He looked between me and Amber.

She pulled out her phone and gave it to me.

"*Hey, Amber, it's Kathrine Anderson.*" It was a text from my mom to Amber. "*Sorry to bother you, but Matt left earlier this afternoon and hasn't made it home yet. He was supposed to babysit for me tonight. Do you or any of his friends have any idea where he could be? Thanks, sweetie.*"

I almost threw her phone back to her as I pulled out my own. "Crap," I muttered.

Eight missed calls and seventeen texts from Mom.

"Is everything alright?" Lucas asked, squeezing my hand.

I couldn't believe this had to happen tonight. "Um, I have to make a quick phone call. Be right back, okay?"

He gave me a sad smile and released his grip on my hand. I walked into the cool night air and held the phone to my ear.

"Karissa!" my mom practically screamed. "Where have you been?"

"On a date, Mom. In a movie," I said, matter-of-factly.

"Your brother is MIA, and the twins are home alone," she said, ignoring what I said completely.

I scoffed. "And I am on a date, Mom. He's fine, and I'll be home at midnight. I promise." I shut off my phone, knowing there would be consequences when I got home.

"Hey, is everything okay?"

Jumping a little, I turned around and smiled at Lucas. "Oh, hey, yeah. Just overdramatic moms."

He laughed and held out his arm. "I know what that's like."

We climbed back into the truck and sat quietly while Lucas dug his keys out of his pocket. "Jonathan says he and Amber have been on five dates, and he didn't tell me once!"

I laughed. "Amber didn't tell me anything either! To think we were their friends."

"Not anymore," he joked as he slid the keys into the ignition.

Nothing happened as he twisted the keys.

He let out an awkward laugh and tried again. The truck's engine gurgled but refused to turn over. "Come on. Come on."

I sat on my hands, not sure how I could help. My arms shivered in the darkness.

"Uh, just a second," he said quickly, jumping out of the truck and lifting the hood. He cursed and kicked the tires a few times. I laughed at his reaction and gave him a thumbs-up.

He sheepishly opened my door. "I got good news and bad news."

"Go for it."

"So the truck ain't gonna start unless I get this part, which I should've done weeks ago, but anyway I saw an auto parts store a few blocks back. Would you be alright if we walked over?" he asked in one single breath.

"That sounds fun," I admitted, accepting his hand and jumping out of the truck.

We walked so close that our arms felt as if they were glued together. The stars danced behind thin blankets of clouds. The moonless night made it feel darker than usual, but streetlamps cheerfully lit our way.

"I mean don't get me wrong, it was a good movie," he said as we walked down the street, "but maybe an actual storyline would be nice."

I snorted. "For real! The only dialogue was—" I pretended I was holding a gun and made gunshot noises.

He laughed so hard his face turned red.

Instead of being embarrassed, I accepted my weirdness and laughed with him. I had never felt so comfortable with someone before.

"Hey, you know, I really like you," he said, nudging my shoulder.

"Well, that was off topic," I joked.

He rolled his eyes and laughed. "You wisecrack."

"In all seriousness, though, I really like you, Lucas," I said, stopping and grabbing his other hand.

"I mean I can't believe this is our first time going out! This is so much fun!" he practically yelled. "You're amazing!"

I blushed but held his tight eye contact. "I've had so much fun, more fun than I've had in months!"

He tilted his head and brushed a loose hair behind my ear. "Karissa, you're the most—"

I let out a scream as hands launched out of the darkness and pulled me back.

"Kari—" More hands grabbed him and threw him to the ground.

Under the dim streetlamp, I watched the men in black masks begin beating Lucas. There were at least four. Their fists and feet were flying against his body. They huddled together, circling him as they gave him no mercy. One of them held me back, one arm around my waist and the other holding my hands together.

"No!" I roared. "Get off!"

The man holding me tightened his grip and put his hand over my mouth.

Purple bruises were already beginning to infect Lucas's face. Blood slipped off his lip and onto the sidewalk. His body was beaten so hard and fast that he was too weak to fight them off. I watched him scream in pain and felt rage fill my body.

Without a second thought, I brought my teeth down on the man's hand as hard as I could. Fragments of his skin and blood seeped into my mouth, making me gag immediately. He cried out and backed up, shaking his hand in pain. I elbowed his nose for good measure and sprinted toward Lucas. The men took a break from his beating and turned to me. Fear filled every available part of my body that wasn't rushing with adrenaline.

They looked me up and down, anxious to fight.

My clumsiness disappeared as if it had never existed. I dodged around their fists, spun around their grabby hands, and slid around their legs. I could see their actions moments before they thrust at me. It was as if they were moving in slow motion. I could feel my body moving but couldn't remember my brain telling it what to do.

"Lucas, run!" I roared

He groaned as he leaned over to vomit maroon fluid.

"Lucas!"

The momentary distraction threw my defense off. One man had an opportunity to attack and took it immediately. His fist flew into my cheek, making me stumble. For a moment, I stood frozen, shocked by the fact I had actually gotten punched in the face. I gathered my balance and held up my hands lamely.

"Stop," I muttered, my cheek pounding in pain.

"Easiest $10,000 I've ever made," the man spat back.

I blinked in surprise. "Wha—"

Bam.

Heavy boots kicked the back of my knees, making me feel as though they were completely blown out. I tumbled flatly onto my back, blinking hard.

The man reached into his coat, seductively sliding a knife out. He knelt beside me. Another man grabbed hold of my hands and held them above my head. I twisted pathetically, doing anything to squirm away. The knife glinted under the streetlight, its blade inches above my chest.

"Any last words?" he asked as if *he* was in an action movie. His finger was drenched in blood, my bite had gone deeper than I thought.

"Let Lucas go." I sobbed. "Let him go."

With a flash, he brought the blade down. It caught the edge of my shirt, barely breaking through before suddenly the man was tackled down. I screamed impulsively, taking a few moments to realize I wasn't dead.

Even the man restraining my hands was shocked. He let go and stood.

I jumped to my feet and backed into the alley wall. The mysterious hero single-handedly defended himself against all five men. His skills were supernatural as he counterattacked each of their violent attempts to hurt him. I forced myself to peel away from the wall and crawled toward Lucas.

"Lucas, p-please talk t-to m-me," I stuttered, my hands shaking intensely as I cupped his face in my hands.

He grimaced, barely hanging on to consciousness. "Kar… Karissa?" Lucas's right eye was completely swollen shut. His nose was cracked and deformed; endless blood ran down into his split lip. I ran my fingers ever so lightly across his jaw, which was now almost the size of a baseball.

I watched my tears slide off my eyelashes and onto his blood-stained cheeks. "That's right, Lucas, I'm here."

"Wha…what happened?"

I shook my head repeatedly. "I don't know. I don't know," I said over and over again.

A thud behind me caught my attention. Still shaking, I reluctantly turned my gaze from Lucas. The hero was standing over all five men, who lay unconscious on the cement.

I was on my feet before I realized I was standing. My entire body trembled so hard that I could barely move.

The man turned to me, his soft face full of concern. "It's okay. You're okay. My name's Cole, Cole Coleman," he introduced himself, touching his chest.

I stumbled toward Cole, desperate for anyone to give me some sort of help or clarity. Tears flowed endlessly down my cheeks and onto my neck.

He held out his arms as if to steady me. "Woah, woah. You're going to be okay."

The next thing I knew, I was hugging Cole, sobbing into his shoulder.

"Karissa, you're okay," he whispered. "I'm going to call someone to help your friend."

"Lucas," I cried.

"I'll call someone to help Lucas," he promised.

I felt a sharp pinch in my neck and my legs began to shake.

"Everything is going to be just fine."

My muscles turned to liquid, my thoughts to mush. "Hmm," I mumbled, collapsing into his arms before I could comprehend.

Cole caught my dead weight. His warm touch felt like heaven. "Relax, Karissa. We'll be home soon."

My body was flipped, and the world was now upside down.

Lucas's hand reached out to me, his words sounding like an ocean current underwater. I tried to reach back and grab his pale hand but felt too weak.

The last thing I saw before I lost consciousness was a white van, with its left taillight broken.

CHAPTER 5

"Are you sure?" Kathrine Anderson's voice shook with emotion. "Unfortunately, yes, but there is hope," the chief of police said, putting the pictures of the crime scene away. "We have active detectives looking for her, and they're not going to give up until she is found."

Kathrine stared at a chip in her wood table. "And the boy, Lucas? He's home?"

Chief Daniels cleared his throat. "He was in critical condition when the first responder found him. As of now, he's in the intensive care unit." The chief watched the woman sob and wished there was something more he could do for her. This was the least favorite part of his job, telling the mothers their children were in danger, especially *this* mother. "We're not going to give up on your daughter, Mrs. Anderson."

The side door squealed as it opened.

Kathrine jumped to her feet, almost tackling her son in an embrace. "Thank goodness. Thank goodness."

"Look, I know I missed curfew, but you didn't have to call the freaking cops." Matt stiffened as all the cops looked back at him.

"They're not here for you, Matt."

"What's up?" he asked, his voice demanding and icy.

Kathrine looked at the chief as if crying for help.

The chief took off his cap. "You should sit down, son."

Matt glanced at his mom before sliding into one of the wobbly chairs. "Is everything okay? Where are the twins?"

Kathrine rubbed her son's arm. "Taylor and Tyler are with Grandma Brooke tonight."

Chief Daniels took the pictures out of the crinkled file once more. He laid them before Matt and cleared his throat. "Around eleven, your sister and her date, Lucas, were attacked in the alleyway of Fifth and State Street. Lucas was found by a postman in serious condition. He is currently in the ICU."

Matt felt his face pale. "W-what are you saying? What about Karissa? Is she here? Who attacked her?"

"The security cameras were taken out exactly twenty seconds before they attacked," he explained. "Your sister has yet to be located."

"What?"

The chief held out his hands as if he was surrendering. "I know this may be a shock—"

Matt jumped out of his seat and looked at his mother. "What do you mean 'yet to be located'?"

Kathrine just stared at him.

"We have reason to believe your sister was kidnapped," he said firmly. He faced Kathrine and held out a piece of paper. "Do you or your son have any reason to believe someone would want to harm your daughter?"

"No," was all she said.

"Any indications of someone who'd want her?" he asked, carefully watching each word.

Matt clenched his jaw so hard he worried his teeth would snap. "What about Dad?"

"Matthew," Kathrine snapped. "My ex-husband loves his daughter. He wouldn't kidnap her."

The deputy next to the chief nodded. "I contacted Mr. Anderson. He has no suspicions of who would take Karissa."

"Could you give me and my son a moment?" Kathrine asked, her eyes bloodshot.

"We should probably get going back to the station, Officer Phillips," the chief hinted.

The officer nodded. "Of course. Call us if you need anything."

The chief led the young officer out of the house and closed the squeaky door.

Matt laid his head on the counter, his body shaking.

Kathrine slowly sat next to her son, rubbing her hand up and down his back. "Oh, buddy."

He raised his head, his eyes staring completely ahead. "I called her ugly."

"Baby, you didn't—"

"Last week, I told her she was stupid for wanting to dance on Broadway. I told her she'd end up on the streets."

"Matt—"

"I stole her charger. I always woke her up after she had fallen asleep. I teased her about Lucas. I never helped her with chemistry even though she sucked," he said to no one in particular, his voice not even a whisper. "And now she's gone."

"They're going to find her. She's not dead," Kathrine promised herself and her son. "She's going to be alright."

Matt's anger grew, and his fingers quivered with furry. "She's not dead."

*****

Beep.

Lucas gasped and sat up as quick as a bullet. Everything was moving too fast and too loud. His head was pounding, his heartbeat in his ears, making it seem like a bell was in his skull.

"Sweetie, lay back," flashes of his mom said softly. "Lay down."

He spun his gaze around the hospital room, feeling as though the walls were shrinking. "The…where…she—"

His dad put his strong hands on Lucas's shoulders forcing him to lay back. "Calm down. You're alright. You're safe."

His face felt like an overblown balloon. "Karissa?" he asked through the wrap that covered the majority of his head.

His parents shared a look. "You need to focus on getting better."

"Where is she?" he demanded, his voice as weak as he was.

Carefully, his mom sat on the edge of his bed, brushing a curl away from his eye. "Karissa is…"

Lucas waited anxiously, his heart pounding as fast as it did when he was attacked. "Where is she?"

"Nobody knows," his dad whispered, putting his hand on his wife's shoulder.

Lucas tried to sit up again. "No, no, I saw her!" He forced his voice out. "Somebody showed up, and then she went to thank them and then…" he stopped short. "And then they took her," he finished, shocking himself as he said it.

"What do you mean?" his dad asked, his face full of concern. "Who took her?"

"I-I don't know," he said, his voice full of guilt.

"Sweetheart," his mom comforted, "we need any details you have. The police are trying to find her. They have no leads."

Lucas laid back, his energy completely gone. "Sh-she hugged the man, and then they were walking away," he said as if it was a question. "She was upside down," he realized. "He was walking away, carrying her upside down."

His mom shot off the bed. "We should call Kathrine."

"We need to call the police, Julia," his dad said sternly. "Lucas has more information than anyone else. We have to keep him talking, see if he remembers what her kidnapper looked like."

Lucas let out a silent sob as he heard that awful word. "They really *kidnapped* her?" he croaked out.

"I'll be back," his dad excused himself.

His mom slid onto the bed, lifting her son's head and wrapping her arm around his shoulders. "Wanna talk about it?"

Lucas looked away, his chin quivering.

"Hey, it's okay," she said softly. "Tell me what you're thinking. Get all those ugly thoughts out of your head."

He stared at her, his body trembling. "I can't believe this happened."

She nodded solemnly. "The hardest thing you can do in life is watching the people you love most get hurt while you sit on the sidelines, doing nothing. But we have to leave this up to the people who can find her."

"Yeah?"

"Yeah," she said, wiping a tear off his cheek. "Life is never going to get any easier, it'll get harder, but because it gets harder, we get stronger. Your girl is strong, and she's going to be okay."

Defeated, he laid his head against the pillow. "Why her? Why would they take her?"

His mom sighed sadly. "I don't know, baby. I don't know." Pulling his blanket closer around him, she began to sing a soft melody.

It didn't take long for Lucas's eyelids to start closing on their own. He laid his head on his mom's shoulder as she continued singing, making this feel like the safest place in the world.

CHAPTER 6

Karissa

"You're sure she's going to be alright though?"

"Absolutely. She's going to be just fine. You're a hero, Dr. Coleman. Without you, Ms. Anderson would be dead."

I shot out of a hazy dreamlike trance as if sleeping was dangerous and vulnerable. My heart pounded fast, a buzz in my brain reminded me there was something crucial I had forgotten. Though my eyes were wide open, I could barely see. My vision was unbelievably blurry. I felt like throwing up and screaming all at once. I moaned in fear softly.

A soft hand held a mask to my mouth, pushing oxygen into my lungs. "Breathe, Karissa, breathe."

I did as he instructed, feeling my pulse slow and my vision clear. The room was a soft baby blue, a calming color. My clothes were replaced by a stiff hospital gown, making me feel exposed. I was lying on a hard white table, no wonder my head hurt so bad—

No.

My memories hit me like a train.

I was in a movie theater one moment, and the next I was holding Lucas as he bled in an alley. We were supposed to be dead, or were we? I couldn't make sense of it all. My hands pushed away the oxygen mask. "Coleman?"

He smiled and nodded. "Are you alright?" he asked, his voice hinting at an Australian accent.

I wheezed in fear and shook my head. "Lucas," I pushed out, "where is he? Is he alive?"

Cole soothed my hair with a loving touch. "All that matters right now is that you're safe, my darling."

I let all the breath out of my lungs and closed my eyes. "What happened?"

"You and your date were attacked. I was walking by when I saw it all happen," he explained. "The men were deliberately after you, so after you collapsed, I took you to the only place I felt safe. Right now, all we are concerned about is monitoring if you're safe."

"And where are we?"

"Coleman Labs," he announced, opening his arms to present himself. "Where science isn't a way of thinking but a way of success."

I pushed my Jell-O-like limbs up and tried to shake the fogginess from my head. "Where's Lucas? Is he alright?"

"Sweetheart—"

Not trying to push back any emotions anymore, I sat up and stared at the man. "Where is Lucas?" I said, my teeth gritting.

Coleman shared a look with the doctor. "Do you think she is stable enough for a quick tour?"

The doctor nodded. "If she feels any fatigue, let her rest," he said stiffly.

"Shall we?" he asked, holding out his arm for me.

Though I was still angry, I accepted his gesture and hopped off the table. My legs let me take control, and with some effort, we began walking.

The walls were all painted the same shade of blinding white, making me wonder how anyone could work here without getting a headache.

"Here at Coleman Labs, we don't just research, we cure," he said as he showed her the scientists in their specialists.

"You're full of cliché inspiration, aren't you?" I teased, trying to enjoy the tour of the beautiful technology.

He laughed and nodded. "So it seems. If you ever need motivation, you know who to go to."

The scientists were touching the 3D models with their hands. Spinning the screens through the air. They picked up tangible pieces of their data and threw them into the model, making them become a part of it.

"Incredible, isn't it?"

"What are they researching?"

He straightened his posture. "Whatever they're interested in as long as it is approved by me. In my labs, there's no specific job list. There are only possibilities of what is achievable."

"So they can literally do anything they want?" I asked, watching a scientist add chemicals to her solution, making a puff of powder explode gracefully.

"Precisely." Coleman led me away from the lab and down more hallways. "You know, Karissa, you are quite a unique person."

I bit back a scoff, trying to remember if I was supposed to be scared or angry. "Is that a compliment or insult?"

"Compliment," he said as if I had said something absurd. "I'm incredibly grateful you're alright after what happened."

I thought back to the night before, blinking back tears. "Why did they attack us?"

"I'm not sure, darling, but I know the police are investigating as we speak," he promised.

"Can I call my mom?"

Coleman paused in front of a large plate-glass window. "We already have, sweetheart. She came by while you were out but couldn't stay long. I'm sure she'll be back soon."

I didn't answer, hurt that my mother chose her job over her daughter.

"Would you like to see what I'm working on?" he asked, smiling like a child.

"I'd love to," I said honestly. After all, he had saved me and Lucas's lives, and the least I could do was act like a civilized person.

We walked past the most advanced technical science I had ever seen. At one point, a woman, who had wheels for feet, asked Coleman to sign something and rolled away. Little crawling bugs swarmed through our feet, polishing the floor as they went. The walls would suddenly change from their blindly white to 3D images of nature.

Incredible was an understatement.

We stopped in front of a black door that automatically opened as Coleman stepped in front of it. He winked. "Facial recognition is not only good for cell phones."

The office was completely different from the rest of the labs. His office was made from pure black opal, every inch was ebony black. It took my eyes a few minutes to adjust to the darkness and begin to pick out pieces of furniture. The lights were red, adding to the eerie room, which felt purposeful. Cold wisps of air encircled my ankles as I followed him inside.

Covering an entire wall were huge TV screens, all showing tragedies from news channels. A tornado in the Midwest, a school shooting in New York, a serial killer in Italy, the rumors of war growing, a kidnapping in Utah, and endless sadness.

Coleman noticed me looking and stood beside me. "Disgrace, isn't it? As humans, the overpowering species of this world, we could create Utopia so easily. Instead, we spend our short years tearing each other apart."

"That's true. It's devastating to watch what goes on," I agreed.

"I'm glad you feel that way," he said with a smile. "You asked to know what *I* was working on?"

I turned from the screens to look at him.

"Ms. Anderson, I plan on eradicating this side of the world. And I'd like your help."

*****

Lucas looked at the dying yellow flowers in his hands; they seemed too cheerful even as they browned. He had given up trying to keep his eyes from puffing; it was a lost cause. With his hand balled in a fist, he hesitated in front of the faded white door.

His mother had told him that this visit would bring him closure, that it would help. Lucas never believed her, but it was better than sitting in the dark room every afternoon.

He knocked.

Matt threw open the door seconds after, making Lucas jump. He dropped his rag and grabbed his friend in a tight embrace. "Lucas," he cried quietly.

"Hey, Matt," he greeted, his voice muffled by Matt's shoulder.

"Thanks for coming," he whispered.

"Matthew, who's there?" Mrs. Anderson called.

Matt released his friend and wiped his eyes quickly. "It's Lucas, Mom. Come on in," he said, opening the door for both of them.

Lucas examined the usually chaotic and fun-filled house. The shades were drawn closed, and no lights were on, making it feel like much later in the evening. Microwaved dinners and dying flowers in vases lined the counters. It was eerily silent.

Matt led Lucas to the living room, sitting next to his mother. Lucas took the armchair across from the pair.

Mrs. Anderson plastered a smile on her face but looked as broken as Lucas felt. "Hi, sweetheart, thank you for coming," she said solemnly. "How are you?"

Matt rubbed his mom's back and passed her a tissue box.

Lucas itched his neck and laid the flowers on the ground. "I'm so sorry," he blurted, his voice quivering.

Lucas's words made something snap in Matt's heart. His soft eyes became filled with rage. "You know, if you hadn't asked her out that night, she would still be here," he snapped.

Mrs. Anderson gave her son a disapproving look but didn't say anything.

Lucas gasped silently but couldn't respond. Matt had confirmed exactly what Lucas had been telling himself. "I know," he barely uttered.

"You know?" Matt spit. "Come on, that's all you got? It's your fault my sister is dead." He scoffed. "I thought you cared about her."

Lucas knew this was just Matt's way of grieving, but his heart couldn't take those painful words. "You know that I do. I will never stop caring about her." He let a stream of tears run down his freckled cheeks. "You have to remember that I was there that night. I was the one who watched her be ripped from my gasps and taken into the night! I have to relive that every single moment of my life. I'm hurting too, Matt."

Matt jumped off the couch and grabbed Lucas by the shirt. "Don't make this all about you."

Lucas looked past him at Mrs. Anderson, who was crying on the couch. "It isn't. It never will be, and you know that better than anyone."

Matt's face crumbled, and he dropped Lucas, sobbing as he did. His chest shook with his cries.

Lucas embraced his friend, sobbing with him. "We don't know she's really gone, Matt. She could be fine."

The rage returned. Matt's face boiled red. He threw Lucas back and scoffed once more. "Yeah, that's right, Lucas. She was kidnapped two weeks ago, and the police are now looking for her *body*, but she's probably fine!" He grabbed a nearby vase and smashed it against the side of Lucas's head.

"Matthew!" Mrs. Anderson jumped up and pulled the boys apart. She shoved her son back and pointed toward the kitchen. "Bring me the first aid kit, now!"

Matt sneered at the two before storming off.

Stars danced in Lucas's vision; blood seeped down the side of his face.

Mrs. Anderson sat Lucas back in the armchair. "Oh, Lucas, I am so sorry. I'm afraid Matt is not taking any of this very well."

Lucas didn't look at her but at the family picture hanging over the fireplace. "I-it's alright. He's said all that I've been thinking these past weeks."

"Why would you say that?" she asked, her eyes soft.

"Because I do know that it is my fault," he admitted. "I know that, and I hate myself for it."

Mrs. Anderson grabbed the boy's hands. "It is not your fault. Yes, she was with you when it happened, but by heavens, that doesn't mean the blame is all yours."

Lucas couldn't contain himself. "It doesn't matter if I was the one who actually did this or not! I will always carry the guilt of her pain for the rest of my life."

She didn't respond.

Matt slid the first aid kit across the floor and put his hands into his pockets. His face was heavy with sorrow. "I'm sorry, Lucas. I am."

Lucas looked at the family, broken, changed forever. "I know, it's okay. It hurts me too, Matt."

He promised from that moment on, his life would be devoted to finding the kidnapper.

His life no longer belonged to him, it belonged to Karissa.

CHAPTER 7

Karissa

I fought to close my gaping mouth. "I'm sorry what? You want my help? Why?"

Dr. Coleman held his hands behind his back and strolled around the office. "Karissa, you are a very unique person. You have defied your instincts your entire life and become a better person for it."

As the "thank you, sir" was about to come out of my mouth, I stopped myself. "My entire life? Dr. Coleman, we met a few hours ago."

He held up a surrendering hand. "My apologies, that sounded creepy. What I mean is after we brought you to the labs, we ran some tests to make sure you were alright."

"Tests?"

"Medical examinations," he clarified. "We learned you should be left-handed but force yourself to use your right."

I looked at my hands. "I had a teacher that would slap my wrists when I tried to write with my left hand."

"You also suffer from greater trochanteric pain syndrome, which should put you on pain medication and make you never want to move again, but…"

"I dance, I have pain everywhere." I shrugged. "The pain I feel is the strength I have coming."

"You don't even want to try to medicate it?" he asked, genuine concern sat in his voice as he continued.

My head began to thump with the rhythm of my heart. "Well, um, my dad got addicted to painkillers when Matt and I were in the fifth grade. I didn't want to know if I would have the same problem."

"And Matt is?"

"My twin brother," I explained.

Dr. Coleman smacked his hand on the desk, making me jump. "Again, baffling! Your mother should have not been able to have children, and yet she had twins!"

"She had to use IUI to get pregnant the first time, and Taylor and Tyler were a surprise," I said absentmindedly. "How did you know that?"

Dr. Coleman filtered through the files on his desk. "You and Matt almost died at birth?"

"Yes?" I backed away from the television screens and faced him. "My mom slipped down the stairs and went into labor early. We were in the NICU for weeks. How'd you—"

"Ms. Anderson, you have defied every odd that has been thrown at you. That is why we *chose* you." His words bounced off the walls, sending a shiver down my spine.

My heart dropped. I felt like dropping to the floor like a child. "I'm sorry, what?" I asked with a chuckle.

"I chose you to be the next breakthrough of humanity." He sauntered forward and held out his hand to me. "Will you join me?"

"Sir, I don't know what you're asking me," I stuttered.

Cole tilted his head, unsure how to react to my answer. "Ms. Anderson, we've been watching you for some time now."

Flashes of pictures and videos of me from my first steps to yesterday in Matt's car appeared on the screens. I saw my parents hold me for the first time. I saw my dad giving me flowers after a ballet. I relived the moment I held the twins after they were brought home.

Everything from birth to yesterday.

Yesterday.

Every moment was recorded from all different angles, even the fight. And he had it all. Every inch of my life was displayed on the TVs in front of me.

I could feel my lip quiver as I turned back to face the doctor. "W-what is this?" I barely forced the words out.

He lifted my birth certificate and grinned. "We've been waiting, Karissa. Waiting for you."

*****

Matt scowled at the well-made bed, with the floors perfectly vacuumed, and the sweatshirts neatly folded. This wasn't his sister's room; this was his mother's version of it.

On the desk in front of him was his phone, open to his dad's contact. The voices in his head argued endlessly on whether this was a good idea or not. The funeral was in less than a week, his dad should be there.

In one swift impulsive move, he clicked the call button and held the phone to his ear. Anxiously, he walked around the room while it dialed.

"Richard," his dad answered.

Matt's breath caught in his throat. In all honesty, he had hoped for voice mail. He sat, paralyzed, trying to force a sound out of his throat.

"Hello?"

Matt snapped back into reality. "Dad, it's me. Don't hang up. I have something important to tell you."

There was a long pause at the other end. "Matthew?"

"Yes."

"How did you get this number?" was all he said.

Matt bit back the angry words he had longed to say since he was fourteen. "It's the same one you had four years ago, Dad."

"Did your mom tell you to call me?" he spat. "Tell her the check is on its way, alright? I'm just a little behind."

Matt walked to his sister's side of the room and picked up the old family photo. He had yelled at his sister countless times to throw it out, but she insisted that Dad was still a part of the family even if he had walked out. "No, she didn't—"

"Great, then you'll get a gift around Christmas—"

His words made something snap in Matt's heart. "Well, Karissa's funeral is on the seventeenth. Don't bother coming." He threw the phone on the bed and stormed out.

Tyler was eagerly chatting with his grandpa, who was showing him his latest magic tricks. Taylor sat on her grandmother's lap, listening to a story.

"Look, I get that it's late notice, but I need the food *before* Thursday morning," his mom said from the kitchen. Papers were sprawled across the dining room table, pictures of caskets and flowers, endless unwritten checks. Her eyes were relentlessly puffy and red.

Matt sat next to her and began flipping through the headstone catalog. Anger began growing in his heart as he scrolled through the options of stone. "Mom?"

"No, the funeral starts at nine!" she continued yelling into the phone. "The lunch is at one."

"Mom."

"One in the afternoon, obviously!"

"Mom."

His mom raised an eyebrow, her warning sign. "What do you need, *Matthew*?"

Matt scoffed and stood. "Never mind."

Instead of what a mother should do, she gave him a harsh look and held the phone back up in her ear. Matt watched the chaos of the house and felt as though the walls were shrinking. The house he had lived in his whole life felt wrong and unfamiliar. He didn't recognize the people in the frames smiling back at him.

Before he knew what he was doing, he threw the front door open and ran. His shoes were untied, but he couldn't stop. His arms were pumping, his feet kissing the icy sidewalk. The sound of his heartbeat pounded in his ears. His lungs were about to explode, but still, he didn't stop.

Tears began streaming down his face, the cold air freezing them on his cheeks. His lips puffed out the air before it relieved the pain in his chest. When the sidewalk ended, he didn't. With legs cramped and stomach twisted in knots, he ran into the tree line.

The sun was disappearing, and gentle snow began to drift toward the earth.

His frozen foot caught the root of a tree and sent him flying into the snow.

"Ow," he cried pathetically. Sobs had overcome him. Matt lay on the frozen ground and shook, his wails unheard by anyone.

He cried all the tears he had saved over the past four years. It was his job, as the man of the house, to be strong, to not show his weaknesses. Now that he was alone, nothing was stopping the emotions.

Matt cried for his dad walking out. For his mom working over eighty hours a week. For never giving Taylor the time of day. For criticizing Tyler at football. For never doing anything for anyone else. For skipping football and never telling his family why. He cried for his sister's disappearance and all the words he wished he could take back.

But mostly he cried because most of that was all his fault. He was to blame.

CHAPTER 8

Karissa

The next few minutes of my life were a blur. Coleman's words of threats and violence were ones I would never forget. He showed me my house but through the view of a sniper's scope. I saw my life one trigger away from death and knew what had to happen.

My legs gave out, and I was guided back onto the white table. My arms were strapped to my side and my legs pinned down. Doctors circled me, arranging their instruments in perfect harmony as if they had rehearsed for this very moment.

Tears made their way down my temple. I tried to brush them with my shoulder but failed. Coleman ran his fingers through my hair and grinned sardonically. "Don't cry. You're choosing this. Just say the word and I'll take you somewhere safe."

"*Somewhere safe*," he said, finally admitting I was truly in danger. How easy would it be to cry mercy and go home? "Though once again, I must reiterate," he continued, "if you decide to opt out, Mom, Matt, Taylor, Tyler, and Lucas will be pumped full of lead before you get home."

I tried to swallow but instead ended up gasping out another round of tears. "I choose this," was all I was able to get out.

"Then let's get started," he said, clapping his hands together and pulling up a chair. "Dr. Odin, the camera if you will."

The table lifted my head so that the camera was aimed directly into my face. I stared right into it.

Click.

"This is trial number twenty-eight. Karissa Anderson, seventeen, female, 117 pounds, five foot six inches, AB-, 130/80, 96 bpm," he said to the camera, gesturing to me. "Ms. Anderson, tell me, am I forcing you to do this?"

I knew what he wanted me to say, but I also knew what the truth was. "No, I am doing this of my own free will."

"Wonderful," he said. "Now, this is the new addition from trial twenty-six, combined with the complete results and vaccines of thirteen," he explained to the camera. "Platelet count and WBC are excellent, same as trial ten. And with that, I believe we are ready to begin."

With the hot lights, the itchy paper gown, the doctors staring, and the camera unblinking, it was only so much for me to handle. I let out a wail. "Please! Just let me call my parents and tell them I'm alright! Let me call Lucas. He thinks I'm dead!"

Dr. Coleman grabbed my chin and gave me a hard look. "Darling, after today, Karissa Anderson will be dead. Today, we welcome Sienna. The saving grace of our humanity."

I turned away from the camera as much as I was able to. "Please don't do this," I whispered so quietly I wasn't sure I'd said it.

The doctor leaned in, his face a mere inch away from mine as he sneered and whispered, "You should be begging me to."

My eyes locked on the syringe clutched in his hand. A sharp bold of panic shot through me, making me nauseous and dizzy. "Don't," I pleaded inaudibly. My limbs lurched uselessly against the restraints cramped tightly.

Coleman held the tip of the needle against my neck, making swallowing impossible. "Listen, sweetheart, if you're going to fight, bite down on this." He shoved a soft cloth in my mouth, triggering my gag reflex. With a soft kiss on my forehead, he plunged the syringe into my neck. "It'll be over before you know it."

For a moment of relief, as nothing immediately happened, I thought it had failed. Maybe I was wrong for his experiment. Maybe there was a way I was immune.

Then all at once, it hit me.

I heard the awful sound of someone screaming; with horror, I realized it was me. A deep horrid paralyzing feeling overcame me. It settled in the roots of my bones and contracted my muscles. It coated me, sealing me tight, and suffocated me from the inside out.

Then came the burning. The singing of every inch of my skin. The searing pain was like fire burning me to death. The burn shot out of my heart, stretching down my veins. In pure fear, I looked at my hands and saw the outcome of the burning. Dark maroon scars were stretching down my arms, covering my body. It was an anxious torture, awaiting death.

With one final blink, I lost it all. Every tear, every smile, every giggle, all gone. I felt all the passion, hope, and feeling drained out of me. It was all replaced with revenge, hate, envy, pride, but mostly pure darkness.

Dr. Coleman, the man who had saved me, replaced the sappy unnecessary part of me with real power, stood before me. "Tell me, Sienna, how do you feel?"

"Thank you for my purpose."

He looked at the camera and grinned. "Trial twenty-eight, successful."

*****

Lucas's mom slipped the black tie around his neck and smiled sadly. "My goodness, you look so handsome. How are you?"

He just shrugged and looked away.

"We don't have to stay the entire time," she promised. "You just let me know when you want to leave, and we'll head out."

"I-I just need a minute," he stuttered.

His mom nodded and escorted herself out.

Lucas sat on the edge of his bed, ripping a tag off his new suit. The day before had been an event for picking a few new suits. His mom had done her best to have it be a day all about him and never stopped telling him how handsome he looked. Now, as he clutched his chest, fighting back his sadness, all he felt was emptiness. Still, he couldn't decide whether being numb or heartbroken was the better option.

No matter what he felt, the nightmares never seemed to cease.

There she was, smiling and laughing like always. His hand wrapped around hers, spinning her around and laughing with her. Then suddenly, she was being dragged away, kicking and screaming as they took her. It was much more exaggerated than the reality, which made it that much worse.

Lucas woke up at least once a night, drenched in sweat, screaming along with the girl in his dreams.

Knock, knock.

"It's time, champ," his dad said solemnly, standing in the doorway.

Lucas rubbed his eyes and joined his father, neither of them bothering to talk. The frost-covered branches and snow lazily falling made the world look like a Christmas dream. Though in reality, it was quite the opposite.

Lucas slid out of the truck, his slick new shoes sliding on the icy parking lot. He refused to believe this was happening. There wasn't even a body. How could they have a funeral?

In the lobby of the mortuary, his dad put a hand on Lucas's shoulder. "It's okay. You can be sad today, son."

It was as if a dam had burst open. Lucas finally realized how important that was. He had to be sad, in case. In case they found her. In case everything was true and she was actually gone. He buried his head into his dad's shoulder.

The classical piece Lucas had watched her dance to was played on the organ, greeting the guests. Most of the school was here. Jonathan and Amber sat together, neither of them moving. Her dance teacher shook her frail body uncontrollably. Lots of her relatives whispered quietly. Her boss from Joanna's sat with his wife and baby.

Everyone was here.

Everyone was crying.

HITTING THE GROUND RUNNING

Everyone was in shock.

Lucas couldn't take his eyes off the canvas picture of her surrounded by flowers. It was the most beautiful shot of her he'd ever seen. Beneath it, engraved in the picture, it read, "*As life must end, love will not.*"

"Thank you all for coming," said a minister from the pulpit. "Karissa Anderson was the definition of passion…"

Lucas didn't hear the rest of the speech, he couldn't. All the stories, quotes, and ballads, all told in the past tense, it was unbearable.

After the final speaker, an announcement was made.

"Since dear Ms. Anderson's body may not be with us today, we have asked the congregation to fill her casket with…special items."

Rage filled Lucas unexpectedly as the words slipped from the minister's mouth.

One by one, the people lined up to put their items in the empty oak casket.

Lucas looked at his mother, who was smiling and handing him a beautifully wrapped package. He gave her a confused look and opened the package. With a gasp and a few lost tears, he stared at the gift. It was the picture from the date, her cheek barely brushing his, her smile lighting up the entire photo. He longed to go back to that moment. "It's beautiful."

Pleased with his reaction, his mom touched his hand. "There's another one for you at home."

Lucas stood and made his way to the casket, his eyes scanning the people in the room. He stopped in the middle of the aisle and looked at the Andersons.

Mrs. Anderson was hysterical. Matt gripped the pew in front of him with white knuckles. The twins sat with their grandparents, silent for the first time.

Lucas glanced at the photo and walked away from the casket. His feet directed him to the distraught family. "How are you?" It was a stupid question.

Mrs. Anderson looked down at her makeup-stained handkerchief. "Better," she lied.

He cleared his throat, sliding into the pew in front of them. "I wish I knew what to say. I'm sorry."

Matt stared at the casket and took a shuddering breath. "Yeah," he muttered.

"Um, I have something for you all," he said awkwardly, handing them the picture.

Mrs. Anderson gasped as she viewed the photo. "Oh, Lucas, it's beautiful. Thank you."

Matt ran his fingers over the frame. "Was this taken that night?"

"Yes."

"Wow," his voice quaked.

Lucas stood, knowing he was overstaying his welcome. "If you ever need anything, just let us know. We're always here for... *I'm* always here for you."

To Lucas's surprise, Mrs. Anderson stood and threw her arms around the young boy. "Thank you. I'm so glad you were with her that night. If I could choose anyone to be with her in those moments, I would choose you."

CHAPTER 9

Karissa

The screens showed the usual chaos of death and violence, itching a fit of anger deep in my bones. I tilted my head and lightly touched an image of the aftermath of a protest.

"Tell me what you feel, dear," Dr. Coleman instructed, watching me with a clipboard in his hands.

I fought to analyze how I felt, which was getting more difficult by the hour. "I feel that if I was there, it would not have happened. If I had been there, no innocent people would have died."

"Very good, my daughter," he complimented, making me swell with pride. "Now, what is the first step you would've taken?"

"I would have to know who was in the right or wrong. It would all be in the details."

"The devil is in the details," he muttered. "How will you save them?"

"Kill the ones that stop me."

He stood, walking around me, lifting my hand and feeling it over. "Marvelous. Absolutely marvelous."

"Thank you, sir."

With a clap of his hands, he brushed away his thoughts. "Alright, get in uniform. I have your first mission for today."

"What is it, sir?" I asked, sliding the tight clothes on.

Dr. Coleman took a long sip out of his red mug, sighing as he did. "I must admit, Sienna, I worry about the psychological effects Karissa will have on you."

"I am Karissa, sir."

He slapped the desk suddenly, making me jump. "Do not say that. Never say that! The whole point of you becoming Sienna was that Karissa would be gone."

My heart shuddered. "Of course, sorry, sir, go on."

"Anyway, there are many things, psychologically, I don't know about Karissa. Your mission is to go to the Anderson home and get this."

I reached out and brushed my fingers over the picture he held out. "What shall I do when it is in my possession?"

"Bring it here, and I shall destroy it. Easy enough?"

I nodded.

"Good, now get going. I'll see you in a little while." He stood and set the mug in its usual place.

The air outside the compound was bitter, and icy rain drizzled from the sky. The town below the lab stared back at me, mocking me for hiding. Little did it know, I was done hiding—Karissa was done hiding. It was time for the world to meet Sienna.

My legs were moving before I had told them to run. Before long, I was sprinting, my lungs easily exchanging the carbon dioxide for oxygen. My muscles, which should have tired long ago, pushed harder, strength I had never been able to experience.

In no time at all, I was standing in front of the Anderson home. Oddly enough, my heart pounded, something that felt like fear. I pushed open the door, making it fly off the hinges and land roughly in the living room.

From somewhere inside the child-infested house, someone screamed and giggled. I followed the awful noise and traced it into the kitchen.

Two young kids sat on barstools, throwing peas on the floor where an overweight dog slurped them up. "Taylor, look at Brady's collar. Do you think it's choking him?"

The girl leaned over the stool and felt the small collar. "Probably, let's just take it off."

"But what—" the boy stopped short when he saw me standing in front of him.

The girl slid off her stool and gulped visibly. "K-Karissa?"

The little boy dashed out of the kitchen and up the stairs.

"You-you're alive!" the girl wailed, running toward me and throwing her arms around my legs. "Mom said you weren't coming back but—"

In disgust, I threw her off my leg and tilted my head.

Her little lips quivered as she got herself off the ground. "Matty!" She sobbed, running around me to an older boy.

The older boy gasped and covered his mouth, his face draining of all color. "Karissa? No. No, it's not you." He walked forward and put his hand on my cheek. "Karissa? You...what happened?"

I scrunched my nose and grabbed his wrist in a tight clutch. "No." In a single swift motion, I twisted it until it snapped and threw him to the ground.

He moaned in pain and held his hand to his chest. "Karissa! What are you doing?" the boy screamed.

I stood over him, my boots pressing heavily on his fingers. "My name is Sienna."

In fear, he slid away from me until he backed into the fridge. "Stop, please stop!"

I grinned sardonically as I had seen Coleman do many times before. "You should be grateful to be in my presence."

"What are you talking about?" he roared.

With a single thrust of my foot, I sent him flying over the kitchen island and onto the coffee table. "I need something. Where's Karissa's room?"

Matt clutched his side and pushed himself up. "Where's my sister? What kind of sick cruel joke is this?" he demanded.

I ignored him and went up the dirty stairs to the perfectly clean room. With great care, I dumped out every drawer onto the soft carpet. Nothing. My anger grew as I ripped the doors off the closet.

I threw down ballet costumes and pathetic tutus. Hangers shattered as I threw down jackets and prom dresses.

Until finally, there it was.

Tied with a yellow ribbon and engraved with Karissa's name was her journal. All her personal thoughts and the key to expanding Sienna was in my hands.

As I was walking out, something cracked underneath my foot. I pulled a shard of glass out of my heel and picked up the broken picture. My heart fluttered unexpectedly.

It was a photo of the date. The night before everything had changed. Back when…when…

When I was weak and vulnerable.

I sneered at the picture and threw it back down.

"Why are you here?" Matt said, glaring at the mess I had made. "Who are you?"

"I told you," I said with a dark grin, "I'm Sienna."

He grabbed my shoulders and shook them. "This is wrong!" Tears streamed out of his tired eyes. "It is wrong to use my dead sister to torment this family. And put down her journal!"

I grabbed his shirt and tossed him into the wall. Storming over to him, I leaned down inches away from his face. "You are right, your sister is dead. How does that make you *feel*?" I asked, sarcastic sympathy oozing out of my voice.

Matt let out a breath, still clutching his side. "Karissa, please… don't do this."

"You really are dense, aren't you?" I said, slapping his cheek as I got up to leave.

"You're a monster, Sienna!" he roared.

I tossed my hair over my shoulder and looked back on the chaos I had created. "I know."

*****

"And Jenessa called to see how you were," Lucas's mom said as Lucas pushed his dinner around. "She's been so sweet to check on you. She even offered to bring some dinner. I told her you were free most Wednesdays and Saturdays and—"

Lucas jumped out of his seat as his phone lit up. "Matt, what's up?"

"Lucas, you need to get over here, now. Someone just busted into our house and trashed Karissa's room," he said without taking a breath. "Not only that, but, Lucas, they looked *exactly* like her. They took her jour—"

"Woah, slow down!" Luas interrupted, feeling his knees wobble. "What did you say?"

Matt let out a gasping sob. "Just get over here, please."

"Okay, okay, I'm coming," he promised as he hung up. "I'm going to Ka- the Andersons', I'll be back."

"Is everything alright?" she asked, her voice tight.

"Yup," he said, snagging his keys and jacket as he rushed out the door. Lucas could barely feel his feet moving as he crawled into the old truck. He couldn't remember starting the truck, driving, or parking, but in the blink of an eye, he was in the driveway of his dead girlfriend's house.

Cop cars and ambulances swarmed the place. Police tape covered the hole where the front door once was.

"Lucas," Matt cried as Lucas stepped through the entryway. The boys embraced each other, Matt sobbing into his shoulder as he was shaking.

Finally, Lucas grabbed Matt by his shoulders and took a good look at him. A deep bruise covered the side of his face, and his torso was encased in a tight wrap. "What happened?"

Matt carefully wiped his eyes, avoiding his bruise. "Someone broke in, but they looked exactly like Karissa, but her eyes were red, and scars were *all over* her body, like veins." His body shuddered with his emotions as he continued. "She threw me into the wall and trashed the room and—"

Lucas couldn't seem to get his breath past his lungs. "Matt, that's im-impossible."

"We caught it on our security cameras," he said with a thick tone.

"What?"

Matt led Lucas into the kitchen and clicked a few buttons on his laptop. He stood back as the video began to play.

There she was. A girl was walking away from the house, her hood covering her head, and a journal in her hand. Finally, she turned back, and Lucas got a good look. She had the same face as her. She had the same figure as her. She even walked like her. But that look in her eyes was nothing like his girl.

"Have the cops seen this?" Lucas's hands were shaking, making the table rock.

Matt nodded fiercely. "But now there's a manhunt for her."

Lucas looked at the cops talking to Mrs. Anderson and ran his hand through his hair. "I can't just sit here, Matt." He stood and made his way in front of the cops.

"I want to help look for her," he told them bluntly.

One officer laughed, but the chief smacked his arm. "Sir?"

"I want to help find Karissa," he announced again.

The chief grabbed Lucas by the arm and took him away from Mrs. Anderson. "Listen, kid, I know your relationship with her. That's too personal."

Lucas balled his fists. "I have a relationship with Karissa, not with that monster."

Chief Daniels grinned slightly, the crow's feet by his eyes nestled into his skin. His deep southern accent could bring a smile to anyone's face. "Are you saying you want to be a cop?"

"If that's what it takes."

"What's your name, kid?"

"Lucas Carter."

The cop held out his hand. "Welcome to the force, Officer Carter. I'm Chief Evan Daniels."

Lucas shook the chief's hand. "Thank you, sir."

He motioned his head toward the stairs. "Why don't you help us check out the scene?" he suggested.

"Really?" Lucas blurted out in surprise.

"Sure, why not?" he said, leading Lucas up the stairs and into the trashed room.

Lucas picked up a shattered picture frame with his bare hands.

The chief handed him a pair of tight blue gloves. "Don't need your fingerprints on those, rookie."

Lucas nodded and put the small gloves on. He picked up the broken picture again and felt his heart shatter with the glass. He shook away the feelings and knelt beside the bookstand and ran his finger over a missing spot. "She took something out of here."

Chief Daniels squatted beside him. "Good eye, Carter. Any idea what it was?"

Lucas just shrugged.

"No worries, we'll figure it out. Why don't you stop by the station tomorrow and we'll talk?" he said, nudging the young boy.

Lucas felt his lips tug upward and realized he was smiling for the first time since he lost his girl. "For sure. Thanks, sir."

The chief and officers walked out, leaving Lucas alone in the room. He looked over her things, thrown and trashed across the room. His eyes fell on her Joanna's work T-shirt. Without thinking, he grabbed it and held it against his chest, inhaling her familiar comforting scent.

"What are you doing?"

Lucas dropped the shirt and whipped around. Matt was standing in the doorway, his face scrunched.

"Um, the chief asked me to check out the room," he stumbled.

Matt nodded, sitting on the edge of his bed. "He told me you were gonna be a cop. What about your football scholarship? You have a full ride to the college of your dreams, man. You can't ignore that."

Lucas stood up. "That stuff doesn't matter anymore. Finding your sister's murderer does."

Matt scoffed. "So you're willing to drop your whole life for Karissa?"

He sat next to Matt and sighed. "I was willing to before she died."

"Wow," Matt said, taking a sharp breath in. "Well, I want to join you. I want to be a cop or whatever it takes to find her."

Lucas shook his head forcefully. "No way. You have siblings to help raise and a future ahead of you. You need to move on with your life."

"I can't move on from this, dude."

"Then just move forward."

Matt smiled and nudged Lucas. "Practice what you preach, oh wise one."

CHAPTER 10

Karissa

"Any complications?" Dr. Coleman asked as I handed him the journal. He looked pleased, making my chest swell with pride.

"My brother saw me," I confessed. "He doesn't believe I'm Karissa."

Dr. Coleman pointed to the chair. "Well, you're not." He untied the yellow ribbon and thumbed through the book. "Excellent, Sienna. This will make our progress so much easier."

I sat in the chair and leaned back. "What are we doing?"

The doctor called his assistants over. "Sweetheart, the injection to create Sienna was temporary. We had to make sure your body wouldn't reject it. We want to do everything in our power to prevent Karissa from taking over."

I bolted up in my seat. "No, sir! Please. Don't let her take over again. She has so much vulnerability. She ca—"

Dr. Coleman put his calloused hand on my cheek. "I know, my daughter. That's why we're going to give you a more powerful dosage. Then I've got an important mission for you."

My hand shook, and my vibrant scars dulled and glowed achingly. I lifted it to show him.

"I know. I know," he said as he kissed it. "We're going to fix it. Now." He clapped his hands together. "You just relax, and we'll take care of you."

With a sharp pinch in my shoulder, I felt my consciousness slipping away. My limbs felt like concrete as I let my eyes close.

Instantaneously, my mind became enraptured by dreams.

I was standing on the edge of two paths, my feet ached, and my chest burned. My body was dripping with blood and rain. Something was wrong, I could feel it in every nerve in my body. At one end of the path, the boy, Lucas, stood, coaxing me to follow. His hand was reaching out, waiting to grab mine. His clothes were disheveled, his hair tousled, and bruises coated his body. He looked…older. A sharp clean beard framed his adult face.

"Please, Karissa, we have to go. Please!" he cried, tears streaming down his cheeks.

At the other end was Dr. Coleman, his hands casually sitting in his suit pockets. His lips were twisted up in a dark sneer. "Dear Sienna, don't be stupid. I warned you what would happen. I saved both of you, and I can take that privilege away. I am not afraid to take back what I gave you."

My heart was torn. If I went with Lucas, Dr. Coleman would kill us both. If I went with Dr. Coleman, the world would never be the same.

A hand grabbed my shoulder, making me jump. I sat up. "Did you fix it?"

"We—"

"We added the second dose too early," a doctor, standing in the back, said quietly.

Dr. Coleman dropped my hand and spun around. "Dr. Hansen," he glared, "mind your words."

"What?" I asked, looking at the pair.

Dr. Hansen became braver. He straightened his back and walked closer. "Your second dosage was injected too soon after the first. It's going to take over your body."

Coleman was fuming, shaking with anger. "That is enough, Doctor."

"No!" he cried, standing inches in front of Dr. Coleman. "She was an innocent teenage girl before *you* corrupted her mind! I will not stand by and watch this anymore."

To my surprise, Coleman smiled. "Very well," he snapped, and two guards grabbed Dr. Hansen's arms. "Take him to the training room."

"No!" he screamed. "You're the psycho! Leave her out of it!"

"Sienna," Dr. Coleman said casually, "follow us, will you?"

I stood without questioning and walked to the right side of the doctor.

"Our next mission I have planned is going to be extremely arduous. You're going to have to prove to me that you can put all emotions aside to do what I say. Are you ready?"

We stopped in the middle of a large empty arena. Thousands of seats sat unoccupied around us. The floor was almost as bouncy as it was soft. I faced the doctor. "I'm ready, sir."

The guards shoved Dr. Hansen to his knees and aimed their guns at his head. He looked desperately up at me, tears slipped down his cheeks. "Please," he said inaudibly, "don't."

Dr. Coleman put his hand on my shoulder. "Dr. Hansen told us, and I quote, 'I will not stand by and watch this anymore.' So we are going to make sure that he does not *watch* anything ever again."

My heart leaped so hard I thought it would fall out of my chest. "What?"

He gestured toward the sobbing man. "Take his eyes out."

I took a sharp breath in, not able to get air past my lungs. Had I heard him right? Maybe I was still coming off the anesthesia. "Sir?"

Coleman tilted his head and looked me sincerely in the eyes. "Sweetheart, I told you this was the moment when you were going to prove to me you were ready for our next step. Put your emotions aside and do it."

I didn't respond.

"If you don't," he warned, "there will be severe consequences."

My entire body shook as I wiped my sweaty hands on my pants. "H-how, sir? How do I do this?"

"However you decide."

I could barely move, my head spun. My hand stretched toward Dr. Hansen as he continued to silently cry. The question of "how" continued to run through my mind as I stuck my finger in the corner of his left eye. Carefully, I pushed more pressure into it. Vomit rose to my mouth when it moved upward and closer to my finger.

"Do it, *now*!" Coleman demanded.

In a single swift motion, I pushed my pointer finger around the organ until it was out, hanging by the optic nerve. The swinging eye stared at me as I fell and stumbled back to the ground. Sweat dripped down my forehead. I felt like I would pass out or throw up or both all at once.

Dr. Hansen just stared at me as he touched the end of his eye.

Coleman nudged my shoulder with something sharp. "You're not done quite yet."

In horror, I looked at what he was holding.

Scissors.

"You see, with the anatomy of an eye, if the organ is still attached to the nerve, it still works," he said casually. "You know what to do."

I took a gasping sob. "Plea—"

"Don't let Karissa take over! You are Sienna," he commanded. "If you're not, there'll be consequences."

Anger snapped through my body. "You keep saying that, but how could you punish me? I have nothing left."

"You forget how I own you." He pulled out a tablet and showed the image of the scope. Lucas, Taylor, Matt, Tyler, and Mom, all through the view of a sniper's viewpoint. "One word and I'll pump them full of lead."

My fingers brushed against the image of Lucas. His head buried in his hands as he sobbed. It was all my fault, all this was my fault. It was time to take responsibility for that.

I clenched my jaw and snatched the scissors out of his hand. Dr. Coleman was right. Karissa was gone, it was all Sienna. Sienna didn't have a gag reflex, Sienna didn't care what happened to her family, Sienna was beyond emotions, and Sienna was stronger than Karissa ever would be.

Swallowing the bile, I grabbed the dry ball and snipped through the thick nerve.

Dr. Hansen screamed with more agony than I had ever heard in my life. Instantaneously, blood began spurting from the socket, more than seemed possible.

"Do the other one, quickly, before he can pass out."

This time, I didn't hesitate at all. I pushed my finger behind the eye and snipped through the nerve in a single moment. Dr. Hansen never stopped screaming. Blood drenched his pale face.

Then it was over. He fell face-first onto the soft floor, his breath stopping as quickly as his cries.

Coleman dragged me back as more blood seeped out from under the doctor. I felt frozen, completely paralyzed. His next words should've made me feel unstoppable, but all I felt was shame.

"I'm proud of you."

CHAPTER 11

Two years later

Lucas straightened his tie as he brushed his back molars. He inspected the toothpaste logo and sighed. He had never liked this brand, yet it was the one he had bought for months. "Oh, well," he muttered to himself as he spit into the sink.

Sliding his boots on, he looked around the messy apartment. Last week was supposed to be laundry week, but then they heard reports that Sienna was back in the country, and he never found the time.

His phone buzzed and let out the familiar three-note ring. "*Press conference starts in 20. Get moving, Luke!*"

Lucas chuckled and opened the text message. "*See you in five then, Phillips.*" The clock on his phone reminded him that he really did need to get moving. Snagging a bagel off the sticky counter, he rushed out the door and into the hustle and bustle of the city.

Within one hundred steps, he was inside the police station, greeted by the familiar smell of the copy machine and strong coffee.

"Cutting it kinda close there, Luke!" his partner, Det. Drew Phillips, greeted.

"Good morning, Drew," Lucas said with a joking smile. "Don't you look spiffy? Is it you or me going on national news?"

Drew straightened his tie and scowled. "I'm your understudy, kid. You hiccup wrong and I'm all over it. Wapah!"

Lucas winked at Drew and lightly hit his chest. "Don't count on it."

"I'm serious though, man," Drew said, suddenly calm as he pushed his blond curls back. "If this is too much, I can step in. It's gotta be hard talking about her."

That struck a nerve, making Lucas want to run or scream or both. Instead, he cleared his throat and itched his clean-shaven beard. "No, it's alright. I can do this. I need to."

Drew put a comforting hand on his shoulder. "Okay, just let me know."

"Pst, Carter!" the chief urged.

Lucas buttoned his suit coat and rushed to his side. "Yes, sir. I'm here, sir. What do you need me to do?"

"Are you sure you're ready?"

Why does everyone keep pushing this? he wanted to scream. "Of course. When do I go on?"

"Twenty seconds." Hands grabbed Lucas and shoved him in front of twelve different microphones. They fluffed his hair, added a touch of makeup, and straightened his tie all in a single motion.

"Sir, you go live in three, two…"

The cameras flashed and zoomed in. He could feel the sweat already building in his beard. "Good morning. I am Det. Lucas Carter. I am the head detective on case twenty-eight. There have been an astounding amount of misconceptions about who she is and what she's doing. Today, it is my job to clear up those misconceptions and answer any other questions you may have."

Immediately, every single reporter, journalist, and blogger in the room began begging for his attention. How was he supposed to choose? "Uh…you?"

The reporter stood, her notepad in her hand and her cameraman standing with her. "My name is April with BME, could you tell us Sienna's story from before she was taken by Dr. Coleman?"

Lucas gulped. When he had been writing answers to potential questions, he refused to admit they'd ask about his girl. "Sienna was known as seventeen-year-old Karissa Anderson. She was kidnapped the night of October 25th. Since being in Cole Coleman's captivity, she has been tortured, brainwashed, and genetically enhanced. She is now going by the alias Sienna, who she believes she is now."

"Detective, what do you mean when you say 'genetically enhanced'?" the reporter continued.

"Uh, I can answer this," their resident doctor stepped in.

Lucas stepped to the side to let him answer. He wiped his palms on his slacks, forcing himself to look like he was listening. In reality, his mind was racing so fast that he couldn't keep track. Drew gave him an inaudible "You good?" to which Lucas just gave an awkward thumbs-up.

"I think that's a good question for Mr. Carter," the doctor said suddenly.

Lucas snapped back into attention. He hadn't heard a single word anybody had said. "I'm sorry?"

A woman with fiery red hair jumped up. "I'm Michelle with *The Cassette*. Sienna has been seen catching bombs headed for schools. She has single-handedly stopped wars in the Middle East. Most people would call her a hero."

Lucas waited for her to go on, but she never did. "Oh, um, I'm sorry, what was your question?"

"Would *you* call her a hero, Lucas?"

"That's Detective Carter to you!" the chief shouted from the back.

Lucas thought about the question and had to separate his feelings from the facts. "Sienna has certainly done heroic things in the past. However, as time has gone on, she's, uh, stopped. Dr. Coleman has turned her into a murderer. She has killed hundreds more than she has saved. Right now, our mission is to take her unharmed and try and get Karissa Anderson out."

The crowd all shouted their next questions. The room was bouncing with energy. The chief shot him with a warning look.

"Detective, once taken into custody, will she be charged on account of her intentional manslaughters or pardoned because of her actions to stop the wars?"

"Detective, what if Karissa has made up Sienna to make herself look innocent when captured?"

"Detective, is it true you have a personal relationship with the suspect?"

HITTING THE GROUND RUNNING

Lucas didn't even want to look at Drew or the chief. He knew how disappointed they were in him. He tried to speak, but no one was listening. He cleared his throat, trying to get them to notice him. Finally, he snapped and slammed his fist on the podium.

The room went dead silent.

"Karissa Anderson was seventeen years old when she was kidnapped by a forty-six-year-old man. That man was Dr. Cole Coleman. Since being kidnapped, he has genetically modified Karissa into Sienna, who is stronger than any man or weapon. It is true that in the beginning, they were working for good. They stopped fighting in the Middle East, rescued hundreds from the Brooklyn fire last year, and even managed to save a plane that was falling out of international skies with three-hundred civilians. Now, they have suddenly switched their ways and are on a killing streak. Together, they've killed triple the amount of people they have saved. Why? We don't know," he said without a breath.

When no one bombarded him with questions after speaking, he continued, "Our job is to find her and get back the girl her mother and her three siblings miss and grieve over." A strong feeling of power filled his chest. "Our job is to take Karissa out of Coleman's creation."

He stepped back from the microphones, and the reporters jumped to their feet. They screamed more questions, but Lucas was escorted out of the room. From behind him, he could hear the chief muttering to himself. Lucas's skin prickled, and he could feel the adrenaline rushing out of his body. The men that were dragging him pushed him into the conference room and backed out.

Lucas turned and proudly faced Chief Daniels. "Sir, I apologize if I overstepped the information I was permitted to share. I didn't think they would be so passionate about her."

The chief held up his hand, instantly silencing him. "I'm not angry with you, son. I just knew if you stayed out there any longer, they would make you the villain." He gave the boy a loving smile. "That's the thing about passion, it creates its own story. People just decide whether that's a good or bad thing."

Without thinking, Lucas threw his arms around his boss and held him as tight as possible. "Thank you, sir."

The chief held him as long as he needed before stepping back and smiling once more. "Most people would discourage you from this case, with the confliction of your relationship with her. I want you on this case *because* of your relationship. Your hope is going to help us find her more than anything else. You know that Karissa is still in there somewhere."

Lucas sighed and looked at the photos of her, stretching across the room. "I just pray I'm right."

*****

"Controversial arguments have been rising since Det. Lucas Carter lost his temper at a press conference this morning," the news anchor said to the camera. "Some say this isn't the first time Carter's emotions have gotten in the way of his professional relationships."

Matt snatched the remote off this couch as he watched his best friend stutter his way through the reporter's questions.

The clip of Lucas was humiliating. He cleared his throat three different times before slamming his hand on the podium and screaming that she was only a teenager when she was kidnapped.

"Lucas Carter has been the head detective on case twenty-eight for the past three months, without so much as a lead on where she could be. So let me ask you, America," the cut back to the shot of Lucas being escorted out of the press room, "is this the person you want handling the serial killer of the century? A naive lovestruck schoolboy? I'm John Rogers with WGS nightly news, good night."

Matt resisted the urge to smash the TV as the next segment of the news was the latest videos of his sister holding a high school hostage.

Tyler ran into the living room, his untied cleats tripping him every step of the way. "Let's go play catch!"

Secretly, Matt clicked the screen off before Tyler could see anything. "Bud, it's freezing. We can go out tomorrow."

The boy dropped the football and gave a look that could make a puppy cry. "You say that every day."

Matt tossed the deflated ball between his hands. "Well, I only work till four tomorrow, so I will for sure," he half-lied.

Immediately, Tyler broke into a grin and took off to feed the obese dog for the third time.

The new side door squealed as Taylor and his mom walked in, their arms full of groceries and backpacks. Taylor slid her things onto the counter and twirled across the kitchen, her tutu brushing the chairs as she spun.

Matt followed her and began putting the food away. "How was your dance class, Tay?"

Taylor perched on the edge of the counter, standing on her tiptoes. "Fan-tab-u-lous! Madame Roussel says I'm the best dancer in the class. She wants me to have private lessons like Karissa!"

The name hung in the air, suffocating Matt and his mom. She gave a sad smile. "Th-that's great, Tay," he said after gathering his bearings.

His mom took a minute to gather herself, turning her back to her son before forcing a smile and returning to reality.

"Hi, Mom, how was your day?" he asked after the twins had sprinted up the stairs.

She set down her bags and patted his cheek. "Oh, Matthew, you're so much help around here. I hope you know how much I appreciate you. You've stepped up tremendously."

Matt shrugged lamely, not sure how else to respond. "Uh, Lucas had his press conference today."

"Did he?" she said excitedly. "I bet he did great."

Matt slid his phone to her, the news anchor, and all her snarky comments echoed off the kitchen walls. Her face went from a full smile to a grim frown. "I need to watch the full thing. Poor Lucas. I wish we could've talked him out of this."

"Oh, we tried, Mom," Matt said quietly. "But you know what, he's happy. He's passionate and he's closer than anyone else."

His mom slid the eggs into the fridge and took a long breath. She was about to continue, but Matt's phone interrupted them.

"Hello?" he answered.

"Is this Matthew Anderson?" the caller asked.

Right after his sister's identity had been released, Matt's family had received so many threatening phone calls they had to change their numbers and throw out the landline. Now, as a new voice asked him who he was, he felt the same familiar panic.

"Depends who's calling."

"I'll take that as a yes," the caller continued. "My name is Det. Drew Phillips. I need your help."

The detective's next words made Matt's blood turn to a frigid slush.

CHAPTER 12

Karissa

At first, the memories consumed me. Every time I saw blood, I could see his face. Each time I caused any harm to any other person, I felt Lucas's touch, heard his soft guiding voice, and smelled his comforting usual scent. I wanted to give in so badly, go home and have him forever.

And then came the looks of disappointment.

My family, friends, and even Lucas would always stare and the blood that stained my skin with horror. Their shame of me was suffocating. Their guilt was crushing.

Dr. Coleman would stand just beside me, urging me to continue. His words of pride and love would ooze out until I promised myself I would do anything to please him. Dr. Coleman always said we had to remove emotions to have the ability to kill another. I disagreed. In that moment when there's a beating heart inside a chest and you have to decide to rip it out, it was never the numbness that drove me, it was the anger, the urge to please, the utter disgust with myself.

Our goal was to show the world how useful I could be and how I could save countless lives. The government applauded me, the military saluted me, the president badged me. I felt like the superhero in the comics my brother had read to me.

After a while, Coleman was forgotten as my creator; he was merely my secretary, my doctor. He was envious and tired of the positive praise we had gotten.

On the way to a mission, Coleman pulled me aside and changed our battle plan. "Sienna, the world is no longer afraid of you."

"And that's a bad thing? They respect me, sir," I said bluntly.

Instead of lashing out, he gave me a fatherly smile and tilted his head as though talking to a child. "If they forget what you're capable of, they will take advantage of you. We need to show them what you are truly capable of."

"How sir?"

The doctor looked solemnly into his laboratory. His demeanor wasn't full of its usual sharpness but rather replaced with joy. "Kill them all."

*****

Lucas set down his ballpoint pen and rubbed his face. After an entire evening of nonstop phone calls, emails, and reporters banging on his door, he had to turn the world off. He had never felt so ashamed. It seemed as though the entire world was disappointed in him.

As he left the station, the chief told him the achievable was only possible with the right mindset. Ever since then, the words rang around Lucas's head like a bell, infesting him. Did the chief expect Lucas to be proud of the press conference? Did he expect Lucas to be confident they would find his girl?

New voice message from Mom.

Lucas picked up the flip phone and clicked on the voice mail.

"Hi sweetie, it's your momma. I just wanted to call and let you know your father and I watched your video on the news today! That was such a treat! I have it on tape if you want to watch it when you come for dinner on Sunday. Speaking of which, why don't you bring your new work friend? What was his name? Drew? Ah, something like that. Anyway, I hope you're doing good and staying warm. Love you, baby!"

He smiled to himself as he listened to the message. At least he knew one person who would always be proud of him. "*Thanks, Mom,*" he typed back, knowing deep down, that she'd rather have him call. "*I think Drew would love to come. See ya Sunday.*"

Kicking off his socks, Lucas peeled back the sheets and crawled into the twin bed. His head pushed deeply into the thin pillow as he reached out and flicked the naked light bulb off.

His apartment was not much more than a closet; heck it was a closet, but it was all he needed. Within a walking distance of the station and the train, his little home was perfect for him.

But as the darkness covered the small room. Everything broke open.

Lucas clutched his chest and let it all out.

Ever since the day she was taken, Lucas hadn't gone a single night without this feeling. The feeling of a hollow, empty, guilt-ridden heart. The endless questions of "What if I hadn't asked her out?" or "Why didn't I defend her better?" His gut was still twisted in anguish about the way he lay on the ground like a pathetic child while she was dragged away.

As if that wasn't enough, over and over again, tormenting him endlessly were *her* screams. The sound of her shrieks would keep him up all hours of the night.

Every single night, she haunted him.

*****

Karissa

Dr. Coleman had asked unimaginable things, but *this*? This was by far the worst thing he had asked. To go back to the most vulnerable part of my past and bring it into my future.

My hands practically froze to the fire escape as I scaled up the apartment building. With each step, my boot made a sharp metallic ring on the rungs of the ladder. Finally, after my toes were frozen to the inside of my shoes, I was standing outside his apartment window.

There he was.

My Lucas.

He was so close.

He looked so peaceful.

I crawled in.

Coleman had made it his personal mission to make Lucas an invader to my mind. It felt as though each second, I was forced to watch the films Coleman Labs had made to prove Lucas was a monster. They contained images such as him with another girl, giving her our story in exchange for his pleasure. Others showed him tearing up our pictures or disgracing my name in front of national news.

They all replayed so many times I almost believed it all.

Until finally, when my hands had been rubbed raw from washing other's blood off, when my tattered clothes were thrown out, when the horrors of my day had cooled, I dreamed of him. I dreamed of his goofy shoulder shake. I dreamed of the way he used his hands to tell a story he was passionate about. I dreamed about the feel of his lips as they brushed my cheek. No matter what they told me, I knew he wasn't the villain in my story.

His hand hung slightly off the bed. His eyes moved under his eyelids, and his breath was quick despite how peaceful he looked.

My heart tugged toward him, but my feet felt glued to the old carpet. "Lucas," I whispered so quietly I wasn't sure I had said anything.

But he sat up, quicker than I thought possible. Before I could do anything, he was standing on the other side of the bed, holding his gun toward me. He blinked hard, trying to get his eyes to adjust to the darkness. I thought that once he saw me, he would run toward me and scream in joy; instead, he raised his right eyebrow and laughed.

He just laughed.

The small gun shook in his hand as he looked around the room, at the ceiling, the walls, the floor, at everything. "Very funny, Coleman! Is this your idea of telling me to drop my case? Well, just like your last epiphany, it's not going to work!" he screamed, which was met by loud banging from the neighbors.

I straightened my back and tilted my head, reminding myself I could do anything. I had to remember who I was and the evil I had done. "Lucas, stop."

When he looked back at me, his eyes were brimming with tears. "This is just sick," he said, his voice shaking despite his confident look. "Get out of my room."

My eyes captured all of him in an instant. His bare chest covered in goosebumps, his hair wild and slightly curled, his shaking body. Everything about him was so beautifully human, so fragile. It didn't help that tears were beginning to spill over his eyelids.

"Don't make this hard," I could barely whisper.

Only a few hours ago, I had twisted a man's neck so forcefully it snapped in half, now I stood in a boy's room, paralyzed like a scared child.

Never releasing his grip on the gun, Lucas stormed across the apartment until he was an inch away from me. I could feel his anger, his sadness, his heat as he loomed over me. "Don't make this hard? You can't be serious. This isn't the first time you've tried this, Coleman. I'm not stupid. I learn from your mistakes."

His words seemed as though they were stolen and put together at random. None of what he said made sense.

"Lucas, will you just come with me? I don't want to hurt you."

He sneered, making my heart pound. For as long as I had known Lucas, I had never seen him convey any emotion besides pure joy and heartfelt kindness. Now he stared at me, with the gun aimed at my abdomen, like he had the capacity to kill.

"I'm not falling for this. You'd think you would learn after two failed attempts of dragging Karissa's image up here, you would learn, but—"

That's it.

In a single move, I grabbed the gun from his fingers and bent it in half. My own rage felt like it was steaming off me. Right as I was going to shatter each little bone in his arm, he gently pushed a piece of my hair behind my ear. My breath hitched in my throat. More tears rose to his eyes and fell down his face.

"Either Coleman's getting more smart or more stupid." His thumb gently rubbed my temple.

I reached up to put my finger over his and felt it.

The scar.

Lucas opened and closed his mouth, trying to force his words out. "The last ones didn't have this," he croaked out.

Finally, I caught on to what Coleman had been doing to Lucas. The sick mind games he had played. I swallowed the lump growing in my throat.

"He doesn't know I have this."

Lucas dropped the gun and backed up, his face pale under the moon's light. "What are you doing here, Karissa?"

Sienna, what's taking so long? Coleman's voice echoed in my earpiece.

"I can't tell you."

His face scrunched up as if it was his only defense against his building sadness. "Is it really you?"

I had so much I wanted to say, so much I wish I could do, but I had made a choice. It was my life for the safety of all I love. Coleman was waiting. I had to hurry. What I had to do would break our trust; he'd probably hate me. But if I didn't do it, my mom, my brothers, my sister, Lucas, his mom, everyone I had ever known would die. At least this way they all had a chance.

"It's me, Lucas. It's Karissa."

He sprinted toward me, throwing his arms around my middle and spinning me around. I let out a single sob, a heart-wrenching, desperate sob.

"It's okay," Lucas said, holding me as tight as possible. "I've got you. You're safe now."

I lifted the syringe and plunged it into his neck. "I'm sorry," I wailed quietly. "I'm so sorry."

He groaned slightly, his body became heavy. I dropped the needle and caught him as his legs gave out on him. My tears dripped off my face and down his cheeks.

"Karissa?" he questioned, his eyes no longer able to find me.

"I'm sorry, Lucas."

His neck fell back as the last bit of consciousness slipped out.

"*Sienna, answer me or I give the snipers my go-ahead.*"

"No," I said calmly. "It's done. I'm coming."

"You have Lucas?"

"Yes."

CHAPTER 13

Dr. Coleman was waiting in his office when I got home. My shoulder ached from carrying Lucas, my heart from betraying him. "I'm proud of you, daughter. I know this couldn't have been easy."

He had no idea.

"Dr. Saunders, if you would, Lucas needs a little energy it seems," Coleman instructed.

I took a seat on the floor, holding my knees to my chest.

"Relax, Sienna. You look weak."

I looked away as Dr. Saunders woke Lucas up. I couldn't bear to see his first reaction to my betrayal.

Dr. Coleman stood in front of him, grinning like a showman. "Welcome to our humble abode. We're excited to have you."

Lucas sat up, took everything in quickly, and spit on Coleman's shoe. "Screw you. You killed Karissa."

I stared at the floor, wishing I could disappear.

Dr. Coleman slapped him hard, making me wince audibly. "I only killed the weak parts of her. I made her unstoppable."

From across the room, I could feel Lucas's gaze, but I still couldn't stand to look at him. "You don't have to feel guilty, Karissa. I know you didn't want to hurt me." His words healed a piece of me I didn't know was broken. Finally, I met his gaze and slightly shook my head. "I know the good is still in you, and I need you."

"Oh, please quit the act, Carter!" Coleman screamed. "You might have fooled the public with your 'help me, my girlfriend is trapped!' gimmick." The doctor was an inch away from Lucas's face. "But you ain't foolin' us."

Lucas didn't buckle under Cole's heavy presence. "So what are you going to do with me? What's the real reason you brought me here?"

Coleman grabbed the back of his neck and pulled him across the floor. "*This*. This is why you're here."

They hung over me, both staring with similar looks but drastically different feelings. "Why, sir?" I whimpered.

"She was such a good sheep," he started, his monologue voice creeping into the conversation. "Did exactly as I told as long as we were helping people, as long as we were doing good." He dropped Lucas's neck and focused on me. His hand curled around my shirt, pulling me to my feet before I realized it. "Then when we decide to go full bad cop, she hesitates. Each day, I could see her resisting more and more. Every disease, war, and storm has an origin, I just needed to dig a little deeper to find hers. Can you guess what it was?"

Lucas was right in front of me, his eyes locked into mine, and this time, I didn't look away. "Her genuine goodness. Deep down, Karissa is still in there. No matter what you do, you can't take out who she is."

"Wrong!" Coleman roared. In a fit of rage, he threw us both onto the floor. "It was *you*," he said, holding up the worn-out journal I had stolen. "It was the lovestruck schoolboy that was foiling all my plans!"

We shared a glance, neither of us knowing what to say.

Coleman's shining shoes clicked on the sleek floor as he paced around us, flipping through the pages. "In every single page, '*Lucas Carter this*,' '*Lucas Carter that*.' He was infesting you from the very beginning, my daughter."

It was as though the ground was crumbling around me, dropping me into a deep void forever. Tears filled my eyes as I watched him tear out pages. His fingers crumpled and tore out each and every heart-devoting page until it was just two covers holding wrinkled edges of paper. "That is why you are here."

Lucas's pinkie lightly traced my hand, reminding me I wasn't falling down an endless hole.

"Mr. Carter, you are the final key to unlocking Sienna's full potential."

*****

"My name is Det. Drew Phillips. I need your help."

"Excuse me?" Matt almost scoffed. "I'm sorry, I think you've made a mistake. Have a great ni—"

"My partner was taken last night by your sister. Do you have any way of contacting her or any idea of where she might take him?" Drew asked breathlessly.

Matt's fingers curled tightly around the phone, his blood felt as though it was freezing him from the inside out. "Who's…" he cleared his throat and started over, "who's your partner?"

"Lucas Carter."

The distant sounds of his siblings laughing, his mom talking on the phone, and the TV trying to sell the newest truck all faded. It was as if all of Matt's senses were ripped out of him. "Lucas…"

There was a pause on the other line. "Matt, would you mind coming down to the station tonight? Any leads you might have would be useful."

Matt looked at the slightly slanted vacuum lines tracing his sister's side of the bedroom. "I'll be right there," he said as he hung up. He slid his tennis shoes and faded ball cap on and slid down the messy stairs. "I'll be back, Mom."

"Matthew!" she called, her voice a warning. "Where are you going?"

"Uh, I forgot to pick up some stuff for Tyler's game," he fibbed. "I promise I'll be back soon."

The feeling in the room shifted as if his mom already knew. She took a seat at the dining table and patted the chair next to her.

Matt stole a wistful glance at the door but sank into the chair beside her. "Mom, there's something I need to do."

She didn't respond, only slightly arched her eyebrow.

HITTING THE GROUND RUNNING

"Lucas was taken by Kari- by Sienna." He stared at the table, refusing to see the look that went along with her gasp. "I talked to his partner, and he thinks I might have some leads to where she took him."

Over the past two years, his mom had been understanding; she'd been gentle, she'd been there. She dropped over half of her work schedule to be with her children as they grieved. No matter how Matt or the twins lashed out, she had been patient and worked it out with them. Now, as Matt confessed, anger and pain crossed her face. Her patience and understanding were wiped out in an instant. "Son, we just got in the groove of things. We just started to hit the ground running, and now you want to dive right into this…drama," she said slowly.

Matt fought his urge to lash out. "She's still my sister, Mom. If I have any chance to help her, I'll take it."

She was close to yelling, tears streamed silently down her face. "Absolutely not! That *monster* is not Karissa. She is not your sister, she's not my daughter. My daughter is dead."

Her words snapped something inside Matt that he'd been trying to heal. "You can't make this decision for me," he said, standing confidently.

"Please," she whimpered. "I can't lose another kid."

Matt whipped around, his heart pounding with adrenaline. "Lose another kid?" he howled. "I can't believe you just said that."

Her hands were shaking as she clutched her chest. "You can't look me in the eye and tell me that you still care about the girl who is murdering. You can't tell me you still call her your sister."

Upstairs, the twins were laughing, their sound of pure happiness brought Matt to tears. "Karissa was the only part of this house that had any passion. She was the only one who did anything for others." He swallowed, trying to steady his shaking voice. "My sister, Karissa, was the only one who truly had hope for me. So forgive me for still holding onto hope for her." He threw the door open. "Keep Taylor and Tyler safe. Tell them I'm bringing their sister home."

"Matt, don't walk out that door," she pleaded.

"I love you, Mom." He snagged the truck's keys and rushed outside.

Outside the police station, Matt looked in the rearview mirror and angrily wiped his tears. He needed to be strong. He needed to be the man of the house.

The heavy smell of paper and doughnuts greeted him as he walked in, his legs shaking. He glanced around the station, dark horrible memories flashing through his head.

"Mr. Anderson!" a familiar southern voice greeted, slapping his hand on Matt's shoulder. "Haven't seen you in a bit!"

He forced a smile and shook the chief's hand. "Good to see you, sir."

Chief Daniels's smile faded. "Matt, what are you doing here? Is everything okay? How's your mom?"

"Matt's gonna help us find Detective Carter, sir."

Matt whipped around and saw the man that sent chills down his spine. "Officer Phillips," he whispered.

"Hi, Matt, thanks for coming," he said with a friendly smile.

This was the officer that was sent with the chief to tell his mother Karissa was gone. The officer that had dropped an atomic bomb on his life. This was the man that wanted his help, ironic. Matt felt paralyzed.

"I'm Detective Phillips, but you can call me Drew." He shook his hand. "Why don't we go into my office and talk?"

The chief gave a nod of approval. "I'm glad you're here, son. We're not ready to give up on your sister just yet. There's still hope."

"Hope," he whispered with optimism in his voice.

Drew led him into a shared office, pulling the chair out for Matt. "Take a seat, get comfortable. Can I get you anything to drink?"

The words flew past Matt's ears as he stared at the adjoined desk. He pushed past the *Lucas Carter* nameplate and grabbed the frame. His sister's smiling shocked face as Lucas pressed his lips against her cheek.

"Hey, if this is too hard, I understand if—"

"You know, uh, this picture was taken like three hours before she went missing," he said, not sure if he was telling himself or Drew.

"This was the last picture ever taken…well until the press took over." Finally, he sat in the seat, not letting go of the picture.

"So is there anywhere your sister would go to get away? Any place she had talked about?" Drew began, a legal pad sitting in front of him.

Matt searched his memories, regretting the conversations they hadn't had in years. Up until the day their dad left, they were best friends. After that, they were merely acquaintances.

"It's alright, take your time—"

"Cosmos Infinite," he blurted out.

Drew scratched down the name. "What does that mean?"

The sudden remembrance of that name sent a jolt of shock inside him. "We were like eight years old. Our parents had been screaming for hours, and we were sick of it. So we snuck out and found this gorgeous, abandoned space museum. We spent the entire day and most of the night exploring it. After that, whenever the house got too loud or Dad was in one of his moods, we would slip out and head there."

Drew was writing down every word Matt said, never asking a question or stopping to look up.

"One day, Karissa had been rejected by her dream dance school," he continued. "She applied as a sophomore, trying to get an early start, but they wouldn't even look at her records. In her mind, it was the end, she was crushed. Mom was on an overnight shift, and the twins were at day care. I didn't even check to see if she was home, I knew where she'd be. And lo and behold, she was at Cosmos Infinite."

Drew dotted his Is and crossed the Ts before looking up, a proud smile plastered on his face. "Perfect. That's exactly what we needed!" he cheered. "Oh, man, yes! Now, I—"

Drew's police scanner crackled, making the boys jump. "C-can yo-you hea-hear m-me, Drew?"

Matt and Drew jumped to their feet and gasped. "Lucas?" they yelled together.

"I-It's m-me," he cried, every other word cutting out.

Drew pounded on the speaker. "Are you alright? Are you with her? Where are you?" he yelled.

"I need you, now."

CHAPTER 14

Karissa

My foot tapped anxiously outside the tightly sealed door. I could take the door down with a single tap, but for a reason I didn't understand, I didn't. So instead, I stood inches in front of it like I was trapped inside.

"Hey, Sienna," Dr. Saunders said as she walked by. "How are you feeling?"

"Fine," I said plainly.

She looked between me and the door. "Is there anything I could do for you?"

My fingers lightly traced the edge of the door handle. "I want to see him. I want to go in."

Her panic was so thick it was practically visible.

"Just for a little while, please."

Dr. Saunders slid her key card against the door and grabbed my hand. "I need you to listen to me."

I stopped walking and looked at her tear-filled eyes.

"I started working here twenty years ago when we were still trying to cure cancer. Coleman's ideas exploded after his wife died. Then he found you, and he became obsessed. He built this lab, he spent billions, to perfect you, the perfect weapon," she whispered harshly. "I wanted to quit the instant he showed us your picture when you were five days old. But if this is the only way to get you out, to get you to fight, I'll stick around."

My heart practically shattered in my chest. "I can't leave now. After everything I've done."

Her grip on my arm tightened as if I was the only thing keeping her stable. "*You* haven't done anything of your own free will. All the bad things that you've done happened after he gave you the serum. None of this is your fault. Nobody's blood is on your hands."

"Dr. Saunders, even if it was possible, how could—"

Footsteps were descending in the hallway behind us. "Whatever you need, Karissa, I'll get it. We're gonna get you out of here." She dashed away.

I watched her disappear, my thoughts running faster than I could follow. *We're going to get you out of here.* More doctors were rooting for me. I couldn't give up now. My hand swung the heavy door open, and I stepped inside.

Every ounce of feeling came rushing back as soon as I caught sight of my guy.

Lucas.

He sat on a bench in a glass cage. His shoulders hunched over his knees, shaking. I couldn't breathe as I realized he was crying. His hands pushed his hair back as he sobbed. As quietly as possible, I made my way to the clear prison.

"I know I've bothered you a lot, especially about this," he whispered to no one, "but I am begging you for just one small miracle, okay? That's all I'm asking for, just one little boost."

My hand was touching the glass before I had told it to do anything. "Lucas?"

He jumped off the bench and sprinted in front of me. "Karissa. It's you."

I half shrugged, my lower lip quivering like a child's. "I want to..." My tongue felt too big for my mouth, making speaking almost impossible. "I wish I..."

He put his hand up against the glass as though trying to hold it. "Karissa, I'm not angry you brought me here. You know I'd do anything for you, right?"

It was as if a magnet was pulling me toward him. I put my other hand to the separation, wishing I could feel his warm touch. "I don't deserve that, Lucas," I whimpered, hating how weak I felt.

His features flashed anger, sending chills down my neck. "Don't you ever say that. You are still my girl, and nothing that you did will change that."

My emotions betrayed me, sending a wave of tears down my cheeks. "The thought of you has been the only thing keeping me somewhat human. You can't believe what I've done." My own voice haunted me. "I'm the epitome of danger and—"

"I don't care!" he persisted. "I love you."

My mouth fell open in surprise.

"Well, isn't that nice?"

From the way Lucas paled, I didn't have to turn around to know who had just entered. My heartbeat rang in my ears, my fingertips tingled, and my feet froze to my shoes.

"I may be an accomplished man," Coleman said confidently as he sauntered into the room, "but I'm not afraid to admit when I've made a mistake."

I pivoted around on the heel of my boot, trying to make it seem like I was still on his side. "Sir? What mistake have you made?"

Dr. Coleman gave me a long look and turned back to Lucas. "I thought having Mr. Carter here would make you heartbroken, angry, maybe even apathetic. However, this young man has done quite the opposite. He's not only turned you into an emotional girl again, but he's trying to convince you to leave?" He clicked his tongue in disapproval. "Oh no, that's no good."

I stole a glance from Lucas, and the world seemed to stop for a precious moment. He gave me a single nod. I returned the small gesture.

"Dr. Saunders?" Coleman called. "Could you do us the honor of telling us what happens to *traitors*?"

"No!" I gasped before thinking.

Dr. Saunders was dragged in, her mangled legs trailing behind her. She barely mustered the strength to lift her head, sending a shock wave of horror through me. I could barely recognize the poor woman. Her sad, bloodied eyes locked with mine. "I…don't regret it…Karissa."

Coleman's face was twisted in anger. "Kill her, Sienna. Now."

The walls seemed to be closing in on me, ripping the air from my lungs. "Sir?" I croaked, my voice barely cracking out any sound.

His shining shoes clacked toward me, the bright vein sticking out of his neck. "You heard me. Kill her."

Dr. Saunders's eyes stared deeply into my soul, whatever was left of it. She gave a nod, not a word slipped from her lips, but the action screamed at me.

"I can't sir," I sobbed. "I-I'm scared."

His fingers wrapped around my shirt, holding me inches off the ground. I could've ripped off his arm if I wanted to, but he must've known I wouldn't. "I did not risk my entire career, I did not spend billions for you to be *weak* and *scared*." His rich words filled me with pure horror. "You have one last chance. And, my dear, I promise you won't like the consequences of your refusal."

I had spent the last two years of my life doing anything to please this man. I had done things that would make people sick. I'd done things to people I didn't think could be done. The endless amount of blood that rested on my hands was evil. But at this moment, the strength Dr. Coleman had given me was finally mine. I held his gaze, and with every ounce of will I had, I muttered, "I will not."

His hand flashed through the air faster than I could comprehend. A sharp pain pinched my neck before I could move. I shoved him back, stumbling as I did. "What'd you do?" I slurred. My vision was going in and out of focus. Lucas's sobs echoed in my head as I sank to my knees.

Everything was moving too quickly. Flashes of my life were playing in front of my eyes at hyper speed. Memories were ripped out of my heart straight from my chest. Hot, burning, white pain encircled me, twisting my organs, scrambling my brain, shattering my bones. I scratched at the scars coating my body, feeling as though they were trying to rip my veins from my skin.

"I'd like to thank you, Sienna. You are the key to unlocking the future. You were the experiment. Now, nothing is holding us back."

My screams threw themselves from my throat. I could feel *everything*. My heart breaking, my sadness drowning me, my happiness overwhelming me, my excitement exploding, my anger overtaking me. I could feel every emotion hijacking me.

And then I felt nothing.

Nothing at all.

*****

"I hear what you're saying, and you're wrong," Matt argued.

Drew looked back at the automatic lock and huffed. "I know, but I've seen enough movies to know that if you shoot a lock, the door is gonna open."

"You shoot it, we're already dead," another officer said in a hushed voice.

Drew's adrenaline was pumping. He had finally made it. The case he had been working on for two years was moments away from being resolved. The only thing holding him back was a locked door, with his helpless friend on the other side.

"So if no one else has any ideas, what are we gonna do?"

"We just need a key card," Matt whisper-shouted back.

Ding.

The group whipped around to see a doctor holding her card against the lock, the door slid open behind her. "You must be here for Lucas."

Matt visibly swallowed.

Nobody replied though a few officers flipped the safety off their weapons.

"My advice? Get the kid out of here and leave her. She's past saving," the doctor warned.

"We're getting everyone out of her," Drew promised her and Matt. "Thank you for your help."

She tossed them her key card. "Stay low."

Lucas sat up slowly as the door slid open, his friends standing confidently on the other side. He smiled without realizing it. "Drew. Matthew."

Drew saluted his partner and gave orders to the officers. "Don't worry, Lucas, we're gonna get you out. Matt, unlock the door and meet me at the entrance."

"What are you going to do?"

Drew tightened his grip on his gun. "I'm going to end this."

"Lucas!" Matt started running toward him but stopped inches in front of the glass cell. "Oh my- are you…what'd they do to you?"

His new injuries screamed at him, a painful reminder of what Coleman had done to her. This wasn't her fault. She hadn't done anything to him.

Matt slid the card in front of the lock and helped Lucas out. "Are you okay?"

Lucas wiped the blood gushing from his temple. "Matt, you gotta get out of here now. This is too dangerous for you. I can't let your mom lose you too."

Matt looked at the gun in his hand with disgust. "I've spent these last years watching you try and bring my sister back. Living in a nice suburban house, letting my mother and siblings pretend nothing happened. I'm done, Lucas. We're all getting out of here." He gathered his courage back and gave Lucas a loaded gun. "Now, who hurt you?"

Lucas wasn't sure how to explain everything. "Listen, Matt, Karissa isn't like before, he's changed her into…how do I put this?"

"He's made her unstoppable," an all-too-familiar voice interrupted.

Coleman sauntered into the room, a smirk on his face and a gun to Drew's head.

CHAPTER 15

There she was, Lucas's girl. She stood motionless. That usual sparkle in her eye was gone, her gaze dull. Her knuckles were still red and swollen from the beating. That wasn't his girl. This was what was left of Coleman's creation.

Matt lifted his gun, his hands shaking. "Drop it, Coleman."

Coleman grinned sardonically. "One simple command and I could make your sister kill you," he egged on, holding a remote dauntingly toward her.

"Shut up and drop the gun," Matt said, tightening his grip.

Lucas looked around the room at every possible scenario. One wrong move and he could kill them all. The puzzle pieces snapped into place as a final thought entered his mind. He lowered the gun and shot Coleman's foot, making the man scream and fall to the floor, dropping his weapon.

Drew whistled, impressed. "Nice shootin', tex. Good to have you back."

Lucas stood over the doctor, giving Drew a knuckle bump. "Good to be back, man."

Coleman saw the boys momentarily distracted and took his opportunity. He reached for the remote and pressed a few buttons.

"No!" someone screamed.

Drew kicked the remote out of his hands and raised his gun.

Lucas barely had time to register what had happened before Karissa sprung from her statue figure and tackled him. Her fingernails tightly enclosed around his throat as she held him down. Her legs wrapped around his, holding them down, her face emotionless, staring down at him. He was defenseless as he fought for another breath.

Drew loaded his gun and aimed it at her.

Matt threw himself in front of them. "Do not shoot her!" he commanded.

"She's going to kill him!" Drew shrieked back. "She's going to kill him!"

Lucas didn't try to fight. "Karissa…stop," he squeaked out. Purple and red dots began dancing in front of his eyes. His hand slowly raised to her cheek, tingling with its lack of oxygen. "Karissa."

Matt dove over Coleman and snatched the remote off the floor. "Drew, hold him down!"

Drew put his foot on the doctor's chest, now pointing the gun at his nose. Matt clicked a single button and watched his sister collapse into an unconscious slump.

Lucas twisted to his side and coughed as the air rushed back into his lungs. "What'd," he coughed, "what'd you do to her?"

Matt shrugged and looked at the device. "Sleep mode?"

Drew watched Lucas push himself to his feet, shakingly. "You alright?"

Lucas just nodded, not taking his eyes off his girl.

Coleman shared his gaze, staring at his unstoppable creation now lying helpless on the marble floor. "You schoolboys are going to ruin everything!" he roared.

Drew knelt next to him, pushing his shoulder to the floor. "How do we get Sienna out of her?"

Coleman straightened his posture; even lying on the ground staring down the barrel of a gun, he kept his stature. He laughed in Drew's face. "That's not how this works, *Officer*."

Matt kicked Coleman's bullet wound, making him scream in agony.

"How do we get Karissa Anderson back?" Drew growled, inches away from the doctor's face.

Dr. Coleman looked back at her, tears brimming the edge of his eyes. "Over my dead body will you destroy my daughter."

Rage filled every inch of Matt's body as he stared into the eyes of a truly evil man. "You'll only wish you were dead," he growled through his teeth.

"Is that a threat?"

"It's a promise."

Again, Coleman laughed, staring Matt right in the eyes. "I've been through things you couldn't even try to imagine. I've made your sister do things that would make you hate her forever. Your words will never scare me, boy."

Drew looked back at Lucas who hadn't said a word. "What are we going to do?"

Lucas slipped his arms under Karissa's neck and legs, carrying her like a child. "We're getting her out of here. That's priority number one. Then we get *him* to the station, get all the information out of him we can. Call the chief and let him investigate the lab."

Drew yanked Dr. Coleman off the floor and to his feet, handcuffing him. "You heard the man. Let's go."

Matt rushed to Lucas's side. "What are you going to do with her?"

Lucas looked down at her face. Her eyes were unmoving, not even an eyelash twitching. He watched his own tear slide down her cheek and whispered, "I'm going to get my girl back."

CHAPTER 16

For as long as Kathrine Anderson could remember, she wanted to be a mom. Every Christmas, she would beg for nothing more than sweet little dollies. The hours of her childhood were put into learning how to nurture her babies and soothe their imaginary cries. Some days, she would simply sit on the floor, stroking the doll's cheek, singing quietly as it "fell asleep."

It took four years of endless tears and negative tests until Kathrine and Richard decided to take a less common route to having children. Sixteen-thousand dollars they didn't have, doctor visits every few weeks, building an additional floor to their house, and finally, they were ready for twins.

Kathrine could hardly contain her excitement. Her whole life, she'd wanted a baby, and now she was getting two. How lucky was she?

Every morning, as the sun would slowly creep through the billowing curtains, Kathrine would lie on her side, gently stroking the side of her stomach, singing quietly to the growing babies inside. In only a few short months, Kathrine would have her desires fulfilled; waiting was agonizing.

Richard left early one morning, worrying about a big work presentation. If everything went according to plan, Richard would come home with a promotion and a six-figure salary.

Just as he was heading out, Kathrine spotted the leather briefcase still resting on the nightstand. She called for him, but he was already out of earshot. Clutching the case, she rushed after him, knowing it contained everything he would need for the day.

HITTING THE GROUND RUNNING

The first stair took her foot perfectly. The second rolled her ankle. The third caught her toes. The fourth watched as she desperately flailed her arms out. The fifth cushioned her knees. The sixth was where her stomach landed, sending shooting pain through Kathrine's entire body. Her screams caught the attention of her husband, who had run back into the house to get his forgotten briefcase.

Kathrine's wails drown out the sirens.

Days later, Kathrine sobbed over her tiny babies. Richard did everything he could to try and comfort his distraught wife, but he knew all that could heal this wound was coddling their children.

Kathrine would spend her lonely hospital nights carefully rubbing the twins' heads, singing softly, lulling them to sleep.

Ten short years later, Kathrine and Richard found themselves once again preparing for another set of twins. Kathrine was tired, working until her feet bled, only to come home to a dirty house, energetic kids with intense after-school schedules, and a cranky husband who seemed to blame Kathrine for the life he didn't want. She wasn't sure she was ready for two screaming sleepless babies to add to the mess. But when her sweet, beautiful kids were finally ready for bed, waiting eagerly in their room for their mommy, it made it all worth it.

That moment when her sweet daughter had run into her mother's arms, feeling as though a nightmare was still chasing her, Kathrine caught her with a warm hug, holding her crying baby, rocking her, trying to soothe the girl. She ran her thumb down her baby girl's cheek, softly singing.

Now, nine more years later, Kathrine stood outside the hospital room, biting her too-short nails. She nodded as if she heard what the doctor was saying, but the words bounced off her ears. Her feelings poured over her heart quicker than she could comprehend, let alone understand.

"Her sedation should be wearing off any minute now. You can go sit with your daughter until she's awake. I can't tell you how overjoyed I am for you. You're finally going to be a family again," he urged with a warm smile.

Kathrine sneered at the man. How could he say that like it was a good thing? "No."

"I'm sorry, ma'am?"

She gave the girl lying in the bed a final look. "She's supposed to be dead."

The doctor didn't respond.

"I had finally started to move on." She laughed through her tears. "We had a funeral for my daughter. We put a *casket* in the ground with her things. We spent our time going to therapists, religions, basically anyone who could counsel us to grieve healthily. They all said 'no parent should ever have to bury a child.' And they're right, but I made it through."

The girl in the room stirred.

"We made it to acceptance, and it was hell, but we made it. We were ready to hit the ground running and jump back into reality months later. Then we saw her. We saw what she was doing, and somehow it made her death the better option!" she practically yelled. Taking a deep breath, she turned to leave the hospital.

"Mrs. Anderson, please I think you need to go sit with your daughter," the doctor said as he listened to the woman ramble on. "She's going to wake up with questions, so much confusion, so much fear. Please, your daughter needs you."

Kathrine spun around so quickly that the doctor's hair flew back. "That…*monster* is not my daughter." She swallowed her tears and glared at the girl wearing her baby's face. "My daughter is dead."

*****

"Please, don't do this, Sienna! Please!" the man wailed. "I have three kids! They depend on me for—"

"Spare me, I've heard that routine one too many times."

"Don't do this! You don't have to do this, Sienna!"

"Of course, I don't have *to. I could easily walk away, leaving you to deal with the death of all your friends. Killing you isn't something I have to do, it's something I want to do."*

"No!"

Bang.

*****

Karissa

A white-hot pain shocked my chest, shooting my eyes open. Everything felt wrong, uncomfortable.

Where was I? Had somebody found Lucas? How many days had it been since the date?"

"Hey."

Lucas stood in the doorframe, holding a mug, its contents blowing steam toward his face. He looked…*older*. A sharp beard traced his jaw as he smiled slightly. His white shirt and dark slacks caught me off guard. I hadn't seen Lucas this dressed up since eighth-grade graduation a few years back. But this felt different. The way he casually threw his sports coat over the armchair wasn't like him. It was like a routine.

"You're okay!" I cheered. I grinned at him, relieved he wasn't dead on that sidewalk, beaten to nothing.

His eyebrow twitched. "Oh yeah, I'm fine. I mean my voice is a little sore, but the doctors said that's normal. It'll be fine in a few days."

"Your voice? I was so worried about you, Lucas!" I almost shouted. "I thought they were going to kill you! But you look…I mean…" I sat up and soothed my hair. My hair.

It was so long and healthy. I swung it over my shoulder, something I'd never been able to do before. A chuckle bubbled out of my throat in disbelief. "Woah, what happened here?"

Lucas scooted his chair closer to the bed. "Karissa?" He put his hand on my cheek, his eyes wide.

"Lucas?" I put my hand over his. "What's going on? How long have I been asleep?" I fought for the right questions. "How long has it been since we went to the movies?"

"T-the movies?" he said with no breath. "The movies!" he cried again, jumping to his feet.

Tears tickled my eyelashes. I hugged my knees like I used to do when I was little. "Where's my mom?" Pathetic for a girl my age to be calling for her *mommy*, I know, but Lucas wasn't giving me any answers.

"The movies!" he said over and over, his tears freely running down his cheeks.

"Lucas, I'm scared! Tell me what's going on!"

His entire body shook, skepticism filling his features. "Karissa, what's the last thing you remember?"

Not being able to stand the look on his face, I closed my eyes. "We were walking down the street, going to the auto parts store because your truck wouldn't start. We stopped to talk, and then these guys came out and started beating you up. One of them held me back, so I bit him and tried to help you."

He didn't say anything.

"After that, it's all kind of a blur," I continued. "I'm assuming they knocked me out or something because the next thing I know, I'm here. You should sit down."

Lucas looked like he was going to faint of vomit or both. "I-I need to call someone." He walked out, looking back at me a few dozen times before getting out.

I continued hugging my knees, crying quietly into the scratchy blankets. I just wanted someone to tell me everything was going to be okay. The room was suffocating; never in my life had I felt so lonely.

My hands caught my attention, and long dark scars stretched up my arms, like veins. My fingernails were painted, shiny, and black, a color I had despised on other girls. I traced the scars up my arm, amazed at how different my body felt.

I felt like a stranger in my skin.

"Woah, slow down, Carter," a deep voice bellowed outside the door. "What do you mean?"

"I mean, she doesn't even know the name Coleman anymore. It's like the last two years were ripped out of her," he whisper-shouted through his sobs. "She doesn't remember anything."

The man was silent for a moment.

My legs flew out of the bed before I told them what to do. I ripped the IVs out of my arm and threw the ajar door all the way open. "Two years?" I demanded.

Lucas and the chief of police turned to me, gasping slightly.

I suddenly felt exposed in the papery hospital gown and backed up. "Um, what do you mean, two years? Who's Coleman?"

The chief gaped and stepped back until he was against the wall. "Ms. Anderson?"

I nodded, hoping he wasn't angry with me.

"Would you mind coming down to the station with me and Detective Carter? We have a few questions for you," he said slowly and softly.

Chills ran down my bare legs. I crossed my arms over my chest, desperately trying not to be awkward. "Is something wrong?"

The boys shared a look.

CHAPTER 17

Drew popped the patrol car door open and dragged Dr. Coleman out.

"Easy tiger," Coleman smirked. "I've still got my rights."

"How 'bout you use one of them to shut up?" he shot back.

Every muscle in his body was as tight as an elastic band, ready to snap. For two years, they'd been hunting down the esteemed Dr. Coleman. Now as he was pulled into the police station, his hands shackled behind his back, Drew felt no closure. There was still something deep inside him, nudging him to keep going, keep searching.

"I'm calling my lawyer the minute I see a phone," Coleman informed the officers.

"Detective Phillips," the receptionist called out, "Chief Daniels would like Coleman in holding room 5. He said he'll be right in and help you get started with interrogation."

"Thanks, Janet. Could you hand me Cole Coleman's files?"

The receptionist handed him a thick folder and didn't look at the doctor.

Drew kept his hand firmly pressed against Coleman's back as he led him down the hallway, the folder sat tightly tucked under his elbow.

Dr. Coleman chuckled to himself. "So what's the plan, Officer Phillips? Are you gonna give me water in a plastic cup and shine a light in my eyes? Are you gonna slam your fist on the table and demand I tell you everything, or should I talk to good cop first?"

"You know we could skip all that and you could just tell me everything you did in that lab," Drew said, playing along. "Why don't I just give you a laptop and you can type it yourself? That'd save me a lot of paperwork."

Coleman looked back and winked at him. "That would take weeks, dear boy. Perhaps months. One might call it a novel by the time it is finished. One could even call it a bible."

"Ah, don't kid yourself, Doctor. Your ideas of grandeur stretch even your own ego." Drew unlocked an interrogation room and led Dr. Coleman inside. "But tell me," he continued as he chained the doctor to the table, "why would someone want to read this 'bible' and follow it? What is in it that is so persuasive?"

Coleman leaned back, nonchalantly, fiddling with his handcuffs. "Seems as though you've become too wrapped in the idea of projects. My lab is not a religion nor is it a cult. My lab is merely a place for brilliant minds to stretch their ideas until they become a reality."

"That is until you force them onto your own projects, is it not?"

The man scoffed. "Pardon?"

Drew flipped open the file. "About twenty-two years ago, that would have been true. You had your scientists doing whatever projects they wanted to as long as it was showing progress and was approved by you. Then you become obsessed with the idea of perfecting humanity. You wanted to, and I quote, 'eliminate the weakness of man.' Correct?"

The atmosphere of the room became heavy as Coleman leaned forward and stared directly into Drew's gaze. "You're missing key details, Officer."

"And what are those details?"

"If I told you, I would be doing your job for free," he argued, returning to his casual smile. "You'd owe me some compensation."

Drew fought his own smile. "You're trying to blackmail me?"

The man just shrugged.

"Could you tell me about 'The Minefield Projects'?" Drew asked, shuffling through the folder. "It didn't last long, did it?"

Coleman squinted at the one-way mirror, deciding what he was willing to share. "Let's just say that they broke the boundaries of expectations."

"That's not helpful," Drew muttered.

Dr. Coleman laughed loudly and slapped the table. "Then offer me something! Good heavens, boy! You are the worst detective I have ever dealt with in my entire life. Is this your first week here, or are you getting college credit for job shadowing?"

Drew straightened his posture and swallowed his words. "Alright, let's go a different direction. You picked Karissa Anderson for Minefield Project 28 four days before she and her twin were born. How did you pick her and know her body wouldn't reject the Minefield?"

Coleman stretched forward to try and read the files. "Those are classified names. Where did you get your information?"

Drew slowly raised his gaze, raising his eyebrow as he did. "This isn't my first week. Now, how did you pick Ms. Ander…" his voice trailed away as the chief threw the door open, with Lucas following close behind. Along with…with…*her.*

"Well, well, well, I did not expect this," Coleman whispered, the showman himself finally bewildered.

*****

Karissa

Lucas held the door open for me, grabbing my hand the moment I stepped through. I smiled at him and tried to be casual, not believing *the Lucas Carter* was holding my hand. My hand!

"People are going to stare, Karissa, but don't worry. They're just as confused as you are," he advised.

I nodded, doubting the general public would stare at me. "What are they confused about?" I whispered back, not wanting to embarrass myself in front of the police chief.

Lucas opened and closed his mouth, but no sound came out. Instead, he squeezed my hand and gave me his best smile.

The chief stopped in front of the receptionist's desk. "Did Detective Phillips get my message?"

The woman nodded. "I told him to head into holding room 5 and wait for you."

"Wonderful. Thank you, Janet."

"What's our plan, Chief?" Lucas asked.

Chief Daniels slid a lanyard around my neck. "We're going to head into a room and talk for a while. Try and get Ms. Anderson here up to speed. How does that sound?"

"Can I call my mom?" I asked, once again pathetically asking for my mommy.

"Soon," he promised. "Alright, lead the way, Carter. We'll take her to interrogation room 5." With a wink, he added, "That's the room with the best comfy chairs."

I smiled, silently thanking him for making me less nervous.

With his back straight and a steady look in his eye, Lucas led us past the lobby and down the hallways. He was right, every detective, officer, or suspect we passed didn't just stare, they gasped in horror and backed up. Whether it was voluntary or a reaction, I wasn't sure. I cowered behind Lucas, who kept me as close as possible to him.

Once we reached the door, Lucas stepped in front of me and popped it open.

"Well, well, well, I did not expect this," the man chained to the table said, grinning like a showman.

The chief's face boiled red. "Detective Phillips—"

The detective jumped to his feet, giving me a bewildered look. "What is *she* doing here? Do you need restraints? I have some extra."

Chief Daniels grabbed the detective and dragged him out of the room, already beginning to discipline him.

"As I live and breathe," the man said smoothly, never taking his eyes off mine. "Miss me already, sweetheart?"

I wrapped my fingers around Lucas's sleeve, cowering under his strong stature.

The man watched me and glared at Lucas, his fingers trembling. "What have you done to my creation?" he hissed. "What have you done?" he roared.

Under my light touch, I could feel Lucas tense up, ready to strike at any minute. "We're leaving now, Karissa."

The man grinned, a smug look taking over his face. "I do believe you mean Sienna."

"Who's that?" I whispered, an odd feeling of jealousy filling my stomach. "Is she your girlfriend?"

He tried to stand, his shackled hands making it difficult. "What did you say?"

I blinked and gave an apologetic smile. "Sorry, I was just asking who Sienna was."

Anger consumed the man. His eyes went wide. His body trembled. His veins grew visible. "Sienna…my baby. My creation!" He took a long breath, channeling his anger at Lucas. "You will pay for this. You will pay for each and every mistake, every pathetic part of your miserable attempts to stop me. You will pay for with your blood."

"If that's what it takes for you to leave my girl alone, so be it," Lucas screamed back. "You don't get to hurt her anymore."

The man turned his full attention to me, ignoring Lucas's threats as he continued to yell. "Ms. Anderson, is it?"

I nodded, keeping my hand on Lucas's.

His smile crept over his teeth, a sickly grin. "My dear, no matter where you are, who you are, where you go in life, who you become, what you remember or not, I will be there. I will be watching you. I will be infesting your life. I will ruin your life. And one day, soon, I will have perfected my final plan, and you will die."

My head was fuzzy. The entire world seemed to tilt and spin around me. Lucas's hand pressed against my stomach, practically dragging me out the door. Once we were back in the hallway, he didn't stop. He kept me blindly following him until we reached a small office with two desks.

Without another thought, I collapsed into one of the chairs. "Could I have some water?" I asked quietly, my voice quivering.

Lucas knelt in front of me. "Screw the plan. I'm going to tell you everything, right here, right now. Then we're going to go back to my place and let you get some rest."

"That sounds nice." I picked a frame off his desk and gasped quietly at the picture inside.

"Where should I start?"

I flipped the picture around and tapped it. "Here."

CHAPTER 18

Matt slid the door open, cringing at the creak he never got around to oiling.

"Tyler?" his mom called. "Is that you?"

He thought about how he had left the house, only a few days earlier. His mother had begged him not to go, and he disobeyed and left anyway. Should he even have come home at all? No turning back now. "It's, uh, me, Mom."

Her feet rushed across the sticky floor as she came to greet him. "Matthew?"

Matt dropped his duffel bag and ran to her, throwing his arms across her frail body. "Mom," he sobbed. "We did it. Karissa is gonna be okay."

She stiffened under his touch. "You're safe, and you're home now. That's all that matters."

"Do you want to go see her?" he pushed. "Lucas is setting up a room for her at his place."

Her hands fell from his back. She stepped back and looked him deep in the eyes. "Sweetie, about a year after your dad left, he sent me a letter. In the letter, he talked about if I ever wanted to talk about what happened or anything, I should feel free to come over and do so."

Matt gave her a look of disbelief.

"I never went. I never even thought about it. Do you want to know why?"

His head bobbed slowly.

She looked around at the quiet dark house, having convinced herself this was what contentment was. "The minute he walked out the door, so did all my love and feelings for him. One second, I was screaming at him to stay and provide for the children we had together. Moments later, I was throwing his clothes into the fire. I erased him and our connections from my head."

Matt thought back to the day his dad left. The burning rage had turned to dark grieving in an instant. The only thing that got him and the twins out of the numb sadness was his sister. "So how does this apply to your *daughter* coming home?"

Her voice lowered as if she was ashamed. "When we found out what Karissa was doing…who she had become…I had to do the same thing in my mind. I had to accept that my daughter was dead and go from there. It's like I told the doctor, death was the better option for her."

"Told the doctor…" he thought aloud. "You went to see her? Did you talk to her?" he asked, somewhat excitedly.

"Son," she sighed. "You're not listening. Karissa died, and that is how she will remain to me."

Matt almost scoffed, his ears ringing from her rage-filled words. "That's your daughter out there."

"No, it's not."

"Mom, how could you even—"

"My daughter is dead!" she roared.

The landline ringing interrupted their conversation abruptly. The pair stared at each other, breathing heavily, rage filling the space between them before Matt snatched it out of the cradle. "Hello?" he demanded.

"Matt?" Drew answered breathlessly. "The chief and I found something. We need you here now."

"Is everything okay?"

The dial tone was the only answer.

*****

Karissa

Lucas's hand on my back was the only thing keeping me pinned to reality. The ground seemed to fall endlessly. The air in his small apartment was suffocating. My breath was trapped in my throat as I shook.

"I didn't want you to hear anything from anyone else. So I figured the whole honest complete truth would be the best option for telling you this. I'm sorry, Karissa," he whispered, his hot breath brushing my neck.

I forced myself to look at him, at the tears brimming the edges of his eyes, the sorrow on his face. "*You're* sorry?" I croaked. "I don't…I should be dead."

"Hey," he almost scolded. "Don't you dare say that. Don't you ever blame yourself for what happened."

We sat on the floor as close as possible to each other. Around us were pictures, case files, news articles, all of what I had done. All the misery I had caused was laid out in front of me.

"Lucas," I said, my tone border lining anger, "I took people's lives. I spent the last two years *killing people*." The words were thick, barely making their way out.

He looked thoughtful as he pondered how to respond. "Do you remember it?" he finally said after a few moments of silence.

I shook my head, rubbing the chills away from my arms. "No," I whispered.

"Then you have nothing to blame yourself for," he assured. "From the minute you were in Coleman's captivity, Karissa was gone. Sienna wore your face. You shared nothing else with her."

My fingers traced an image of "Sienna," her hands drenched in dark blood, a sneer plastered on her face, darkness in her eyes. "Lucas, what do I do? Everyone thinks this was me! Everyone thinks I am a ruthless superhuman serial killer, and technically, they're right!"

He looked past me, through the dirty window, and began to grin. "Wanna do something fun?"

I half shrugged, not being able to look away from the list of casualties.

"No longer an option, come on!" He stood and threw me over his shoulder with ease.

Giggles erupted out of my throat as his shoulder dug into my stomach. "What…are you…doing?" I laughed.

Lucas threw the door open, snagging our coats in the process. "We are gonna have fun darn it. Even if it kills us."

"Where are we going?" I said, peering at my bare feet upside down.

"The cemetery," he answered casually.

The bitter air stung my nose as he stepped outside, ignoring the odd looks we were getting as we laughed. "Ah yes, just where I go when I want to have fun."

"Trust the process, missy," he snickered back. "You see, when we had your…'funeral,' they put special items in your casket. Technically speaking, they all belong to you. So we're gonna go get them."

"You didn't let me get shoes, sir."

He didn't answer, but I could tell my comment stumped him. He spun around and grabbed a pair of his dress shoes, holding them up for me to see.

"Ah yes, just my style," I teased.

Lucas snorted and took off in a dead sprint, adding in his own theme music. I laughed and let my body go dead weight.

Within a minute we were standing in front of a headstone. *My* headstone with *my* picture and *my* birthday.

Karissa Sage Anderson
"As life must end, love will not."

"Kind of surreal seeing your own grave," I admitted.

"I don't think many people could say that." Lucas nudged my arm with a shovel.

I accepted the shovel and shoved it into the ground. "Only me and the ghosts."

He laughed, instantaneously bringing a smile to my face. "Only you and the ghosts," he agreed.

What felt like a week ago, I was waiting anxiously day and night for Lucas Carter to send me a text. Now, we were grave robbing at three in the morning, laughing like an old married couple.

"So tell me about prom, finals, graduation, police academy!" I edged him on as we continued to unearth the grave. "I feel like I've been in a coma for two years."

Lucas laughed and cringed through his teeth. "Oh, Karissa, I did so bad the last few months of high school. My teachers were so tired of it that they put me in online school so I could still graduate while starting the police academy. But lo and behold, I did get my diploma."

Ignoring the jealous rock sitting in my stomach, I smiled at him. "So you just blew through the fun parts?"

He stopped digging for a moment, resting his chin on the top of the shovel. His eyes were deeply locked on mine. "There were much more important things, Karissa."

Fighting my blush, I focused my energy on the hard *clunk* noise my shovel had just made. Anxiously, I dug faster, harder, suddenly excited to see what was inside. "This is a beautiful casket," I commented awkwardly as the entirety of the grave was uncovered.

Lucas lay on his stomach, reaching onto the foot of the coffin to find the sealing key. With a twist of his wrist, the lid swung open. Before I could even see what was inside, Lucas swore and put his arm around my middle as if a reflex.

I leaned over his protective stance to look inside.

All the items Lucas had described were gone.

There was nothing inside the oak coffin, except a single handwritten note.

Karissa Sage Anderson. I've graciously emptied this lovely bed for you for, alas, you shall be needing it very soon, my sweetheart.

Forever with love,
Dr. Cole Coleman

*****

"*This is trial number twenty-eight. Karissa Anderson, seventeen, female, 117 pounds, five foot six inches, AB-, 130/80, 96 bpm,*" the doctor said to the camera. "*Ms. Anderson, tell me, am I forcing you to do this?*"

"No, I am doing this of my own free will."

"*Wonderful,*" he said. "*Now, this is the new addition from trial twenty-six, combined with the complete results and vaccines of thirteen,*" he noted, his assistants writing anxiously behind him. "*Platelet count and WBC are excellent, same as trial ten. And with that, I believe we are ready to begin.*"

"Please! Just let me call my parents and tell them I'm alright! Let me call Lucas. He thinks I'm dead!"

Matt leaned back from the video, not being able to watch his sister scream in turmoil.

The chief paused the screen and turned to the boy. "You don't have to watch this, son. It only gets worse from here."

Matt straightened his posture and angrily wiped his tears. "No, I want to see. I want to help Karissa in any way possible."

"Ready to go on, Drew?"

The detective finished scrambling a few extra notes and nodded. The video resumed.

Dr. Coleman was becoming violent and began spouting out his threats. "*Darling, after today, Karissa Anderson will be dead. Today, we welcome Sienna. The saving grace of our humanity.*"

"*Please don't do this.*"

The doctor leaned in, his face a mere inch away from the girl's as he sneered and whispered, "*You should be begging me to.*"

Matt gripped the edge of his chair as Coleman held the tip of the needle against his sister's neck. With a soft kiss on her forehead, he plunged the syringe into the vein. "*It'll be over before you know it.*"

Drew stopped breathing as the sounds of screams echoed through the speakers. The shrieks and wails as the girl withstood the pain encasing her.

The chief slapped the space bar, pausing the video. "I've seen enough. Phillips, show Mr. Anderson what we found under Coleman's personal files."

Drew slid his notes across the chief's overly cluttered desk.

"Holy s—"

All of Matt's expectations flew out of his mind as a picture flashed on the screen. All these years, Coleman was thought of as a soulless monster, a person with no backstory. But here he was, kissing the top of a woman's head as she coddled two newborn babies. Tears slipped out of his tightly shut eyes.

Drew continued swiping.

The next photos were of Coleman and his family, living as any normal family would. With his daughters on their first days of school. With his wife buying a new house. With his family holding a yellow puppy under a Christmas tree. Playing with toys, doing laundry, setting up a swing set.

"H-how…I…what?" Matt finally spit out.

Drew spun in his chair to see Matt's reaction. "Seems as if he lives the classic suburban life, right?"

"Right."

"So why would he suddenly invest everything he had into perfecting the human race?" Drew pressed on, raising his eyebrow with an inquisitive frown.

Matt shrugged, looking at the chief for help. "He wasn't content in his life? He was bored? Anxious? Confined?"

"Quite the opposite," Chief Daniels motioned to the screen. "The doctor was living the dream life. He had two beautiful daughters, a great job, a wife who loved him, and no financial problems. What else could he have wanted?"

Drew tapped the mouse, changing the mood in the cramped office.

"Oh," Matt whispered quietly.

Suddenly, all the pictures were filled with forced smiles and tear-stained faces. The girls asleep in the sickly mother's arms. The girls decorating bandannas for her head. The family moving into a small house in a shady neighborhood. IV tubes, hospital gowns, and doctors.

Fewer pictures of the family and more of messy note pages began to spot the files.

"Have you read his notes?" Matt asked, squinting to read the handwriting.

Drew slipped off his reading glasses and tossed them on his lap. "We've tried. It's as if they're written in another language."

"The lab is doing their best to understand them, but even they are baffled," Chief Daniels added.

Drew continued to click through more pictures. "All that's left of his family is a few scattered pictures of his girls."

"But about seven-hundred photos of Karissa. We're talking about anything from birth certificates and driver's license to prom and dance recitals," the chief said reluctantly. "There is not a single aspect of her life he wasn't a part of."

"So what's the timeline here?" Matt asked, unable to look at the screen anymore.

Drew pushed his chair to the whiteboard resting in the corner. He spun it around to reveal a cliché detective board, filled with pictures, documents, and red string. "If the dates on Coleman's laptop are correct, his wife got sick about nineteen years ago. Immediately, Coleman launched into the Minefield Project."

"He was going to cure her," Matt whispered, his mind buzzing. "The Minefield Project was to cure his wife, and he accidentally made a perfect weapon."

The chief stood and looked at a large space between Drew's string map. "What 'bout this? What are these dates?"

Drew fumbled through his own notes. "Uh, we're not sure. This was right after his wife's first hospital trips and when he started Minefield. There are no documents for six months."

Matt typed in two names onto Drew's laptop. "I bet they have answers."

The men gathered around the screen to see the Coleman girls.

"You've got to be joking," Drew sighed.

"We've got a six-month hole in our research, and these are the missing links!" Matt argued.

The chief folded his arms and nodded sternly. "Anderson is right. We'll go meet the Coleman girls. But first, we need to check up on your sister, Matt."

Matt swallowed hard. "Why?"

"I just got a call from a local restaurant," he almost whispered. "They say they've spotted Sienna."

CHAPTER 19

"Hope you packed your toothbrush and pajamas," Officer Addams said as he led Coleman down the cold hallway. "You're going to be here for a while."

Coleman fidgeted his wrists in the tight handcuffs, ignoring the stupid joke.

"You have a family, Cole?" he continued.

Letting out a long sigh, the doctor turned and gave the officer a passive-aggressive smile. "You don't need to worry about getting to know me, kid. I won't be here long."

"Oh?" Officer Addams asked nonchalantly. "And what is that supposed to mean?"

The pair stopped in front of cell twenty-eight. "It means I'm booked! I have a lot to catch up on, so I'll be out of your hair by suppertime." Coleman scanned the officer for nitty-gritty details. "You'll be back home to Margaret in no time."

The officer almost dropped his keys and slowly raised his head. "What did you say?"

Coleman looked as innocent as a child. "You heard me! I said Margaret and your sweet boy William will want you home for supper."

"How do you..." his voice trailed off. "Don't talk about my family."

Coleman casually leaned against the bars of his cell, still waiting for it to be opened. "And why's that, sonny? Got some trouble at home? Is that a sensitive subject for you?"

Officer Addams slammed his hand beside Coleman's head.

"Officer! Stand down!" ordered an officer sprinting down the hallway. "Now!"

Coleman gestured toward the officer's finger shaking over his gun's trigger. "Is that your knee-jerk reaction whenever tensions are high? To fight? To hurt? Is that why Margaret took William and left you?"

"How the hell do you know that?!" he roared, spit flying off his tongue and onto Coleman's nose.

Cringing at the spit clinging to his face, Coleman grinned sardonically. "Is it that gun around your belt that *triggered* her?"

The officer running down the hall was almost caught up, still screaming at Addams to calm down.

Addams's finger twitched closer to the trigger, his body trembling.

"Am I being too precise? Too correct?" Coleman cocked his head, confidence filling his already large ego. "Am I right on the *bullet*?"

Officer Addams launched forward, grabbing Coleman by the shirt and lifting him a few inches off the ground.

"Now I know how your poor wife Margaret felt. Maybe if you had spent more time at the marriage therapist instead of Joe's bar, she wouldn't be camping out at her mother's house."

"You're a sick man."

"Addams! Release the prisoner! He is unarmed! That is an order," the officer demanded.

Officer Addams glanced his way, trying to make a decision. "Officer Johnson, he knows things…" he whispered. "He knows everything without asking a question…"

Coleman took the split second his mind was preoccupied to make the final twitch, sending his unlocked handcuffs clattering to the floor. At the same moment, he kicked the gun out of Addams's holster and caught it single-handedly. Both officers raised their hands and backed up in surrender.

Officer Johnson glanced at his own gun.

"Ah, ah, ah," Coleman clicked his tongue. "I wouldn't do that if I were you." He laughed as if he was having the time of his life. "You boys around here have got to keep your cool."

Officer Johnson abandoned his gun idea and sprinted toward Coleman, wrapping his arms around his middle and tackling him to the ground. The gun in the doctor's hand fired reactively as they fell. Somebody screamed. Officer Johnson ripped the gun out of Coleman's clammy grasp and slapped his handcuffs back on him.

"I hope you rot in here!" He looked back at Addams. "Were you hit?"

Officer Addams rolled on the ground in pain, blood gushing down his arm. "My shoulder!" he wailed.

"I'll take that as a yes," he replied as he shoved Coleman into the cell, carefully making sure the door was locked behind him.

Once the officers had been escorted away from the scene, a quiet voice echoed. "How'd you know all that?"

Coleman, who was looking out his small, barred window, with his hands laced behind him, carefully twisted his head.

The prisoner across the hall was eagerly looking at the doctor. "How'd you know everything?"

"A magician never reveals his secrets."

"I'll give this week's newspaper if you tell me," he urged. When there was no reply, the prisoner cleared his throat. "Dr. Coleman, we're dying to hear all about you."

"'We'?" This time, Coleman turned to see every prisoner in earshot pressed as far out as their heads would fit to listen.

"Tell us about Sienna."

*****

"I have three questions," Tyler said as he watched his twin pile clothes into a duffel bag. "What are you doing? Can I come? And do I need my light-up shoes?"

Taylor didn't look up as she answered. "Going to find Karissa, yes, and yes."

Tyler stopped short inches through the doorway. "You're what? You can't be serious."

She looked up, the maturity in her eyes looked alien to her young face. "Ty, I am tired of being lied to. First, she's gone forever, now she's home, and we're not allowed to see her. I want answers." Her thumb traced over the worn-in ballet slipper. "I want my sissy back. So I'm going to Lucas's, and I will bring her home."

Tyler looked at his sister, who had seemed to age a decade in the last two years. "Why?"

She huffed and turned her complete focus to Tyler. "He has Karissa. Mommy says she's sick, but not so long ago she was 'dead.' We need to see her for ourselves."

"I don't think this is the best idea," he admitted. "Maybe I'll hang back and cover for you.

"No, you're coming."

"Why?"

With a zip and a slam, she threw the bag over her shoulder. "Because we are eight years old, and we're not allowed to go anywhere alone. So we're going alone together. Besides, you like Lucas. He'll be happy to see you."

Tyler turned and shoved an old pocketknife into his bag. "Fine, *but* I am only coming to protect you. Got it?"

"Got it." Taylor grabbed what looked like a pile of laundry and threw it out the window. The laundry sprung out, becoming a makeshift rope made from the twins' sheets.

"Who are you?" Tyler whispered as she began climbing down, the duffel bag almost bigger than her. He swung his leg out and carefully began climbing down beside her. After three near falls, a few carpet burns, and a rough landing, Tyler landed beside his sister. "Why did we go out the window?"

"Would you like to see the look on Mom's face when we tell her we're going to see Karissa?" she shot back, her tone sharp.

The day was beautiful. The sunlight bounced off the light snowfall, making it feel like a Christmas dream. As they walked down their familiar sidewalk, Tyler looked back at the house, growing smaller behind them.

"How long are we going to stay with Lucas?"

"We'll stay until Karissa is ready to come home," Taylor said sternly. "I won't be lied to again."

A large white van noisily pulled up beside the twins, its left taillight shattered. The van groaned as the man inside manually cranked the window down. "Hey, sorry to bother you. I'm running late for a meeting, and I think I'm a little lost."

Tyler stepped in front of his sister and plastered a grin on his freckled face. "Oh yeah, where are you headed?"

"I'm supposed to be meeting Lucas Carter. I've—"

"We're going to see Lucas!" Tyler announced excitedly.

"Tyler!"

He whipped around and rolled his eyes at his twin. "You can't seriously think we can walk ten miles. And that's *if* we remember where he lives."

"I'm sorry, I need to get going," the man urged. "If you guys could help me out, I'd appreciate it. But if you'd rather walk, I could figure it out!"

Taylor was anxious to see her sister again, maybe that's why she felt like she had a rock sitting in her stomach. Her hands fiddled around her large duffel bag as she debated. "Okay," she finally agreed, hesitantly. "We'll help you."

"Wonderful!" The man jumped out of the van and opened the doors for them, grabbing their bags in the process.

Tyler took one step inside the spacious car and froze. "Taylor… run," he said in a stern whisper.

"What?"

The door slammed behind them. Hands launched at the pair. Taylor tried to scream, but a cloth covered her lips. Her heart pounded as she was filled with panic. Tears slipped down her cold cheeks. It didn't feel real.

Tyler closed his eyes and did whatever he could to get away. He scratched and bit like a toddler, but there were too many. They were too strong. He felt like a child as they wrapped his hands and feet in zip ties. His throat grew sore from his endless wails.

"You liar!" Taylor roared. "You filthy rotten liar! I want my sister! I want Matt!"

"Don't worry, you'll see Karissa very soon," he promised, his voice sending chills down Taylor's back. "Very soon."

CHAPTER 20

Karissa

"I told you this would be fun," Lucas said with a smile.

My fingers spun the straw around my drink anxiously. I just nodded, not wanting to crush his spirits. "You were right."

"It was breaking my heart to see you cooped up in that apartment," he said as he dumped pepper onto his potatoes. "Besides, if anything will get your mind off everything, it's good food."

The steam rising from my soup was getting slower by the minute. I stared into it, seeing my reflection stare back at me. "So what are the scars from?" I asked, rubbing the lines that coated my body.

"You know, I'm not actually sure," he admitted. "You've had them since the first sighting of Sienna. The assumption is that it's a side effect of the Minefield serum."

My eyes locked on him. He was once the kid next door. The boy in high school that gave me butterflies with a simple smile. A silly crush. The football star. The highlight of my diary. Now he was the man who had dropped his whole life for me. The man who had risked his life to save mine.

Who was I? Was I still the girl with a crush on a boy? Was I a woman infatuated with a man? Was I a murderer, a victim, or nothing?

Goosebumps covered my arms as Lucas's hand enclosed my own. "Hey, cute girl, where'd you go?"

I shook away my thoughts, forcing a smile. "Just enjoying good food with good company."

"Is your soup okay? We can get you something else if you want." The endless look of concern on his face suffocated me.

"Oh, it's great!" I overemphasized. "Just trying to…adjust."

Lucas covered my hand with both of his. "And I will be there every step of the way. I promise. You're my girl."

My grin overtook my face. I looked down to hide my blush. "I'm your girl."

He raised my hand and gently kissed the top of it. "That's right. No matter what happens, you're my girl."

I couldn't believe it. Lucas Carter, *the Lucas Carter* had just called me his girl! I wanted to say something just as meaningful back, but I couldn't. My body froze as I stared at him.

He caught my eye and broke into a grin. Tucking a hair behind my ear, he put a hand on my cheek. "You're so beautiful, Karissa."

I leaned in close, feeling as if gravity was pulling me like a magnet. He closed his eyes. I held my breath. My hand was on his chest. His fingers were in my hair. We were a moment apart.

"Everyone get out!" a woman suddenly screamed, her voice echoing across the restaurant.

The building fell silent in anticipation.

The manager rushed to the woman's side. "What's the matter? Is everything alright?"

The woman was pushing her children behind her, her finger arched in front of her as she shook. "No, it's not alright!" she continued to scream. "That's Sienna! Somebody call the cops."

Lucas's hand dropped from my cheek to my hand. He helped me to my feet and tossed his suit coat off his side, flashing his badge. "Ma'am, please—"

The woman refused to be reasoned with. "She is a mass murderer! A wanted criminal! Get her out before she kills us all."

Lucas's whole body moved with his heavy breaths. "Ma'am, please. Sienna has been gone for over a month now." He turned to look at me, giving me a nod. "But this beautiful girl here is Karissa Anderson. She is not a murderer, criminal, or whatever else you'd like to accuse her of. My girl is back, and if you ever insult her like that again, I promise I will not be so nice next time."

The woman tilted her head, her heels clicking on the slick tile as she walked toward us. "Excuse me? You actually believe her insipid lies? You don't think she remembers the blood on her hands?" She was less than a foot away, her accusing finger still pointing directly at me. "You killed my nephew. You looked him in the eye and laughed while he died."

My body trembled, cold tears brushing my eyelashes. "I'm so sorry," I whispered.

Now it was her turn to laugh. She leaned as far over Lucas as she could and laughed in my face. "You're sorry?"

"That's quite enough, ma'am," Lucas said sternly. "Leave her alone."

A crowd was forming around us.

"What are you doing?" Lucas demanded as two men wrapped their arms around his torso. "Let go!" He was being pushed away and held back.

I felt like all the air was being sucked out of my lungs. I wanted to run, scream, hide, but I couldn't even blink. Soon it was just me and her, standing in the middle of the restaurant while everyone stood and watched.

Lucas was screaming at the men holding him back, but they wouldn't budge.

Her hands wrapped around my shirt, dragging me closer to her. "You don't deserve to live after all you've done."

The crowd let out a sound of general agreement.

"Karissa!" Lucas roared.

"I'm sorry," I squeaked out again.

Her eyes wandered across the half-eaten food on our table. Her fingers wrapped themselves around Lucas's steak knife. She looked at it like a child would at a shiny new toy. "What's stopping me from killing you myself right now?"

I took a shuddering breath as I heard Lucas's gun load.

"Drop the knife, right now!" he ordered. "Drop it or I'll shoot!"

She whipped her head to look at him. "I need answers! I need to know why she gets to live but my family doesn't! Why should you live when a child shouldn't?" She placed the knife against my throat, her hand shaking as she did so.

"Drop it!" Lucas continued to yell.

"Tell me!"

I closed my eyes, just for a moment, fighting to remember anything from the past two years. Nothing would come. Nothing but fear and unexplainable guilt. "Because if you kill me," I started, a pathetic quiver in my voice making me sound weak, "you'll be no better than Sienna...than me."

Her grip tightened, making me flinch back in reflex.

"If you kill me, you're one step closer to being the person that murdered your family. That's all it takes," I continued, fighting the urge to cry. "One moment, one heart-wrenching moment overtaken with the wrong emotion to lose humanity. Save yourself from becoming the enemy in your story."

She took a step back, looking at the knife resting in her hand.

I let out a breath.

"You don't deserve to be happy," she said, her own tears slipping down her cheeks. "You don't deserve to live."

Lucas stopped screaming and lowered his gun.

My body felt limp, useless. I rested my hand against the table. "I know and I'm sorry."

The rage returned to her heartbroken face. "Stop saying that!" she dropped the knife and snatched the untouched bowl of red soup. In an instant, she tipped the bowl over my head.

Lucas fired his gun toward the ceiling, pushing through the crowd. The rage on his face would have made even the strongest men cower.

The crowd was in an uproar, all screaming and fighting to get out. Even the woman seemed surprised by what she had done. She took a bracing step back as the bowl slipped off my head and shattered on the ground.

I stood in the middle of it all. Hot soup dripped down my face and began seeping into my shirt. My senses shut off. I couldn't hear anything, my hands felt numb, and the world blurred in front of me.

Lucas threw his sports coat around my shoulders, bringing me back to reality, the awful sticky reality. With one arm wrapped around my shoulders and the other kept tightly on his gun, he hustled us through the restaurant toward the door. The crowd parted like the Red Sea. They were filled with either fear or sympathy, and I wasn't sure which was worse.

Police lights and sirens greeted us as the door swung open. Lucas tightened his grip on me, his breaths deep and heavy.

"Detective Carter," the chief called.

Lucas's head whipped around, his body trembling. "Not now."

I pathetically wiped the red sauce from my nose. "Lucas, can we please go home?" I sniffled, wanting nothing more than to collapse in a heap of tears.

"Detective Carter!" the chief yelled again.

"Not. Now," he growled through his teeth. "You want a report? Talk to the restaurant manager or the crazy lady who tried to kill Karissa. We're leaving." He ushered me into the car and slammed the door shut.

*****

Officer Mia Mills whistled happily to herself as she walked down the halls of the prison. Her key ring swung around her finger, eagerly waiting to be used. She ignored the calls the prisoners made as she passed their cells. No matter what they said, she was free and living her best life while they were caged like animals.

When she reached prisoner 28's cell, she stopped and leaned against the bars, her whistling ceasing. "Good evening, Doc," she greeted, dragging out the vowels.

Dr. Coleman was sitting on his bed, his back facing the door.

Officer Mills banged a key on the bar, making an infuriating metallic noise. "Hey, Doc, you want another chance to talk?"

The doctor didn't even twitch.

"Hey!" she called. "Look at me when I talk to you! I am offering you another chance here."

The image of the doctor glitched entirely.

The young officer didn't take another second to think before sliding the key into the lock and storming in. Once she was in the cell, the doctor sitting on the bed disappeared. She turned and saw a light bouncing off her stomach. When she moved, the image returned to the bed.

"What the…"

Coleman swept his leg under her feet and raised his weapon, a broken piece of his porcelain sink. "Why hello there love." He thrust the piece into her side, twisting it as he plunged it in.

She howled in pain, reaching for her gun. Coleman kicked it out of her holster and snatched the handcuffs instead. He raised her hand and dragged her to the bars, chaining her down.

She looked up at her hand dripping with her own blood. "A hologram? Really, Doc?"

The doctor grabbed her forgotten keys and gun and spun them around his finger. "What can I say? I'm a fan of the classics, Officer."

"You expect everyone to let you just let you walk out the door?" she yelled, desperate that someone else would hear her.

Coleman, who was just about to walk out of his cell, spun on his heel and crouched beside her. He loaded the gun and held the barrel just below her lips. "You don't know me at all, do you?" He laughed, a genuine laugh as if he was thoroughly enjoying himself. "Dear Mia, you have no idea how hard I've worked to get this far."

"You call killing your wife working?" a masculine voice shouted.

Dr. Coleman stood and smirked. "Drew? Miss me already?" He turned to meet his eye, not flinching at the sight of Drew's gun aimed at Coleman's head. "Son, you have no idea what you're talking about," he shot back, a hint of anger creeping into his voice. "I did everything I could to save her."

"Where is she then?"

The doctor cocked his head slowly. "My, my, you guys really do think I'm stupid."

Drew copied Coleman's actions and cocked his head. "I don't believe you. I think you *tried* to save her and ended up killing her faster than the disease could."

The smile faded from Coleman's face. "Watch your tongue, young man. You're overstepping your knowledge."

"Then prove me wrong!" Drew shouted.

Coleman looked up at the security camera hanging on the ceiling and gave it a slight nod. "I could stay here and argue all evening long, but I have lots of work to do. So if you'll excuse me." He jammed two pieces of clay into his ears just as a sharp ringing noise erupted over the PA system.

Drew dropped his gun and fell to his knees, covering his ears with his hands.

Officer Mills tried to cover her ears with one hand, screaming in pain.

"Don't worry, sweetheart," the doctor said, pulling her to her feet by her hair and shoving the gun against her chin. "I didn't forget about you." He yanked her head back and fired.

Drew continued to roll on the ground, shoving his fingers into his ears to block out the noise. The prisoners around him all shared his pain, roaring in agony.

Dr. Coleman spit the officer's blood out of his mouth and ripped her badge off. "Have a nice day, Ms. Mills." Spinning once again on his heel, he sauntered out of the cell and down the prison's halls.

He shoved the main entrance doors open with gusto and took a deep breath, letting the cool air fill his lungs. "It's good to be free," he whispered. "Mr. Anderson, you've outdone yourself once again," he complimented, shaking his friend's hand.

Richard Anderson grinned, soaking in the words. "My pleasure, sir." He offered the doctor a handkerchief.

Dr. Coleman used the napkin to finish wiping the thick blood from his face. "How's phase two coming along?"

"Very well, sir. The twins are on their way to the compound now," he informed, standing stiffly.

"Wonderful," he said, taking one last look at the prison. "Then let's go make sure they get a proper welcome."

CHAPTER 21

"Well, we don't look intimidating at all," Drew said sarcastically as the trio made their way to the front porch.

The chief looked back at Matt and Drew. "Maybe you're right, Phillips. We don't want to overwhelm these girls."

Matt shrugged and took a step back. "I'll wait in the car and let the official detectives do their work." He fake saluted and walked awkwardly back to the patrol car.

Chief pounded on the door and shared a nervous glance at Drew. "How're your ears doing?"

Drew lightly touched them, the ringing in his head never ceasing. "It's better. The doctor said there's nothing they can do about the tinnitus. I just can't believe he escaped."

"Did you talk to Officer Mills's family?" he asked solemnly.

Drew nodded and looked at the ground. "Yeah."

"I'm sorry, Phillips. I should have been there," he admitted.

"No, he would've killed you," Drew said sternly. "Right now, we focus on relocating him and what he's up to."

The door flew open, shocking the pair. Kids ran rampant around the small living room, a dog barked as it chased them, waking a baby which immediately began crying. The girl standing in the doorway looked them up and down, folding her arms across her chest. "Can I help you?" she asked in a sour voice, her gum rolling across her tongue.

Drew's jaw dropped open as he looked at the girl. He was suddenly so aware of his mouth and the lack of spit.

"Detective, close your mouth, you look like a cartoon character," the chief whispered. He straightened his posture and smiled at the girl. "Good afternoon, ma'am. I'm Chief Evan Daniels. Is your mother home?"

The girl's expression fell dark. "How dare you."

"Pardon?"

She scoffed, raising her eyebrows. "Is this some sort of joke?" she snapped.

Coleman pulled his scribbled notes out of his pocket and glanced at them. "This is the Coleman residence, correct?"

"Yes," she said plainly.

Drew continued to stare, not moving an inch.

"So your father is Dr. Cole Coleman?" the chief asked quietly.

She huffed and slammed the door shut.

The men shared a look, absolutely baffled by what had just happened. "What-uh…what do we do now?" Drew muttered.

The chief didn't hesitate to knock on the door once again. "How about this time you use your mouth for conversation instead of gawking."

Drew cleared his throat and nodded. "Yup, you got it, sir."

The door slowly opened this time, and a different girl with similar features greeted them with a smile. "Well, hi, there, sorry about Hope, she's a little rough around the edges."

"She's perfect," Drew mumbled under his breath.

The girl held out her hand and confidently shook the chief's. "I'm Harmony. How can I help you?"

The chief seemed to relax with Harmony taking charge. "Hello, Harmony. My name is Chief Evan Daniels. Is your mother here?"

Harmony's breath hitched in her throat. "Oh, um, why are you here?"

Drew shoved his freezing hands in his pockets. "We're working on your father's case. We believe your mother may have answers for some missing links."

"My father?" she asked, a hint of skepticism in her voice. "Why don't you come in before you freeze to death."

The boys said their thanks and walked into the cluttered house. Drew cringed as his boot crushed a small toy truck. He picked it up just as the truck's owner spotted him and burst into tears.

Hope ripped the toy out of his hand before he even realized she was there. She scowled and picked up the crying child.

"I, uh, sorry," he muttered as she stormed away. Drew shook the horrible experience from his head and took a seat next to the chief.

Harmony handed the chief a framed picture. "My mom and dad were so happy. They were the world's greatest love story, so when she got sick, he fought with everything he had to save her."

Drew peered over the chief's shoulder to look at the photo of young Dr. Coleman and his wife. He whipped his trusty notepad out of his pocket and began scribbling. "When you say he 'fought' to save her, what do you mean by that?"

Harmony picked up a throw pillow and began fiddling with it as she talked. "It's no secret my dad is a genius. He told us her getting sick was the universe telling him to put his mind to work. So he threw himself into the lab work. Instead of cherishing the time he had left with her, he convinced himself he could cure her."

"And did he?" the chief asked quietly.

"My mother was the very first Minefield subject," she said casually.

Drew and the chief shared a terrified look. "He used the Minefield serum on your mom?" Drew almost screeched.

Harmony looked confused. "Dad created Minefield for Mom. Minefield was supposed to be the cure." She took a long breath. "At first, the Minefield worked perfectly. She was spending less time at the hospital, started working around the house, she even started singing again. But only a few weeks after that, the side effects started."

"Side effects?"

Harmony's optimistic expression turned serious. "Blindness, schizophrenia, rageful fits."

Drew flipped a page and continued writing. "What did she see while she had schizophrenia?"

"She talked to a lot of people. Neighbors we didn't have, the 'milkman' who she claimed came every day. Some days she'd answer the door and talk to nobody for hours."

"Did this happen before or after she lost her vision?"

"After."

Hope marched into the living room, throwing her hands up. "Harmony, what are you doing? They asked about Mom!" she screamed.

Harmony stood to face her, keeping her gentle spirit calm. "And I'm telling them."

"Why?" she demanded.

"Because, they know about Dad," Harmony declared, getting a shocked reaction from both Drew and the chief.

Hope faced them, a wild look in her eyes. "What do you know about him?"

Harmony cupped her hand around her sister's ear and whispered something to her.

"Uh, what do you think we know about your dad?" Drew asked uncomfortably.

Hope gave him a smirk and crossed her arms once more. "Everything we don't." She plopped on the couch.

Harmony nudged Hope as she sat beside her. "My sister would like to apologize for her behavior when you first came."

She gave a petty fake smile. "I'm sorry I refused your unnecessary entry into my house for no reason other than to pry at our past."

Drew nodded and gave too big of a laugh. "That's funny!" He coughed and tried to smile again. "Ah, you're funny."

She narrowed her eyes. "Wasn't supposed to be."

They sat in silence until the chief cleared his throat and continued talking. "So your mother and her side effects. Did they get worse, better? What happened?"

"Mom got dangerous," Harmony said, cautiously looking at her sister.

"What do you mean by that?" Drew asked, writing once again.

Hope sighed. "She blew off the handle, that's what she means. She would scream for no reason, throw shelves down, get mad at really little things."

"One day," Harmony chimed in, "Hope talked back to her about doing the dishes, and everything changed. Her eyes became black, and her skin got wet and slimy. She picked up Hope and threw her across the kitchen like she was a paper airplane."

Hope pulled her shirt down to show a long thick scar.

"What happened then?" Drew asked, bewildered.

"Scales covered her body," Hope was almost yelling. "She grew at least three feet, her teeth became sharp, and she let out this animal roar."

"And then?"

"She ripped the kitchen island in half, screamed again, and left forever."

The chief blinked. "How long ago was that?"

"Seven years next week," Harmony said solemnly. She picked up one of the running screaming children and held them tightly.

"And your dad," Drew continued after a moment of silence. "He gave your mom the first Minefield and then…what?"

Hope gave a disgusted look at the mention of her father. "He was there when she changed. When she ran out, he took one look at us and took off after her. Haven't seen him since."

"Except on the news, of course."

"Wow," Drew said breathlessly. "I'm so sorry."

Hope looked fed up. She leaned back and crossed her legs. "Alright, we gave you what you asked for. Where's our side of the deal?"

"Hope!" scolded Harmony.

The chief nodded. "No, she's right. Bring on your questions, and we'll answer what we can."

"Okay," Harmony said nervously. "All over the news, we've seen the girl, Sienna. What did my dad want with her? How did he know her?"

"Her name is Karissa Anderson, she's safe now."

Hope pursed her lips. "So you found her, have my father in custody. Has he said anything about us? Is that why you're here? You think we're involved in all this?" she asked, her voice accusing.

Drew cringed and let out a small chuckle. "Well…your dad escaped…last night."

Hope shook her head. "Oh, joy."

The chief's phone dinged. He slid it out of his pocket and gasped. "We need to go, now."

Drew popped off the couch and shoved his notebook in his pocket. "What's the problem, sir?"

"Kathrine just called the station. Taylor and Tyler have been missing since yesterday afternoon," the chief reported, his voice shaking.

Drew cursed. "Well," he said, facing the girls, "thank you so much for your time. What you've shared with us will make a great difference in this investigation. If you think of anything else," he looked directly at Hope, gathering twenty seconds of courage, and handed her his card, "call me."

To his surprise, blush raced to her cheeks. She looked down at where their fingers met and fought a smile. "I will, thanks."

"Detective Phillips!"

Drew caught up to the chief just as he was leaving the cluttered house. "Sir, what did—"

Matt jumped out of the patrol car and held up a large messy piece of paper. "I figured it out! I know what Coleman wants…woah what's wrong?"

Chief Daniels put his hand on the young boy's shoulder. "We need to get to your house, now."

*****

"It's good to be home," Coleman announced as they entered the compound.

Richard Anderson caught the doctor's coat as he tossed it absentmindedly. "Sir, the twins are in your lab."

Dr. Coleman gave Richard a peculiar look. "You're still on board, Mr. Anderson?"

"Of course, sir. Just as I told you eighteen years ago, I dedicate my life to you and your studies," he said with a pleasant smile, hoping the doctor didn't notice his twitching eye.

"Not to me," the doctor winked. "To the future! To the unstoppable future."

Richard slid his key card against the lock and slid the door open.

"Let us go, you dirty rat!" Tyler screamed as soon as the men entered.

Taylor's lip quivered. "Daddy, please…"

The twins were lying on matching tables, their arms and legs shackled down. Coleman glanced at Richard, trying to gauge his reaction.

Richard walked to their side and put his hands on their shoulders. "I know you want to go home, Taylor. But everything will be alright, and it will all be over soon." He snapped on his latex gloves and lifted a syringe filled with a thick black serum. "It will all be over soon," he repeated.

Coleman slid his camera in front of the twins and sat between them. With a grin and a click, he started the video. "This is trial number twenty-nine. Tyler Anderson, eight, male, sixty-seven pounds, fifty inches, B-, 119/79, 99 bpm," he said in a single breath. "Taylor Anderson, eight, female, fifty pounds, forty-seven inches, A+, 122/84, 104 bpm."

Tyler forced himself to lean closer to the doctor. "If you put one finger on me or my sister, this won't end pretty."

Coleman looked up at Richard and burst into laughter. Richard laughed with him, a genuine belly-jiggling laugh. "Oh, sweet boy," he said, once the laughter had died down, "you're even more adorable when you're angry."

"Mr. Anderson, when you're ready," the doctor urged, holding up his syringe.

Together, the two placed the needles on the edge of the twin's necks and plunged the thick liquid out. Tyler gripped his restraints so hard that his knuckles shattered. Taylor closed her eyes and screamed, her high-pitched wails shattering the light bulbs. The dark serum traveled down their veins, making the light blue blood turn obsidian black. The two kids thrashed on the tables, their movement so violent the leather restraints flew off the tables. Taylor threw her eyes open, black ink filling the usual white cornea. Tyler scratched at his body as scales began to replace his skin. The kids flew off the tables as their bodies outgrew them.

Within seconds the twins were ten-foot monsters, towering over the doctors. Their backs were hunched against the ceilings. Taylor snarled, showing tens of rows of razor-sharp teeth.

Richard looked at his children and fell pathetically to the floor. "Monsters," he whispered, his body trembling in fear.

Dr. Coleman, on the other hand, jumped happily. He clapped his hands together and held out his arms in front of the twins. "My children! My beautiful children!"

Richard shot Coleman a peculiar look as the words fell out of his mouth with triumph.

The twins sauntered toward him, growling and clicking as they shuffled near him.

Dr. Coleman couldn't have been happier. "Rejoice, my beautiful children! You have reached your fullest potential!"

Taylor leaned toward Coleman and snatched him in a single motion, her fingers curling around his middle as if he was a doll. She stood and held him inches away from her face.

Dr. Coleman cleared his throat, his confidence and pride wiped away in an instant. "Why, hello. This is, uh, this is a good angle for you, my dear," he stuttered awkwardly.

Taylor smiled, revealing her endless rows of teeth, curling in toward her throat.

"Hm, very beautiful smile." Coleman chuckled, his voice trembling.

Tyler raised his enormous hand, smiling with Taylor.

Sweat beads trickled down Dr. Coleman's nose. "That's a wonderful hand, son."

Tyler tensed, forcing claws as long as machetes forced their way out of his knuckles.

Coleman paled. "That's, uh, that's great, son."

Tyler raised his claws and slashed them across Coleman's face. Coleman howled in pain, blood instantly gushing out the wounds. Taylor roared back at him and threw him at the wall like a rag doll.

Dr. Coleman crumpled to the ground, screaming and holding his face in his hands. "Richard! Inject them with the Dormir!"

Richard, still dumbstruck by the twins' transformation, slowly stood. "What?"

Coleman peeked out of his hands to see the monsters shuffling toward him. "The sleeper serum, Anderson!" he cried.

Richard sprinted to the tray filled with all different colored syringes. "Which ones?"

Coleman could feel the monsters' cold drool sliding down his back as they lurched over him. "Anderson!"

"What color are they?" Richard yelled back.

Tyler's fingers curled around Coleman's legs, ready to rip them off at any moment.

"THE BLUE ONES, RICHARD!" he screamed.

Richard snatched the blue syringes off the table and plunged them into the giant eight-year-olds. They dropped Coleman and snarled at Richard. Richard fell to the ground as they towered over him. He crawled backward, his hands shaking so bad he thought he might lose control over them. Taylor let out a roar and lunged at him, passing out inches in front of him. Tyler pushed through the fatigue; he threw an entire table across the room before collapsing into a heavy heap.

Richard crept over to them, breathing as quietly as possible. "H-how long will they be out?"

Coleman forced himself to sit up, still wincing and holding his face. "A few days," he said gruffly. He looked at the monsters unconscious on the ground and laughed. "I did it! I made two more unstoppable beasts!"

Richard nudged the creature with the edge of his shoe. "We just knocked them out, they're not completely unstoppable."

Coleman glared at him for ruining his moment. "We used the only thing on this earth that could possibly stop them or anyone with the Minefield. And besides, that was my last dosage. So, Mr. Anderson, they are indeed unstoppable."

He looked at the twins, a smile creeping on his face. "They are pretty incredible. Where's the original?"

Coleman set up a small mirror on the edge of the counter. "Give me one second and I'll take you to see her." With precise ease, the doctor pulled a needle and thread up and down, stitching the large scratches perfectly.

Richard watched awkwardly, not knowing how else to help.

He tied the last knot and smiled, despite the new scar stretching from his chin to his forehead, crossing his nose, lips, and eyebrow. "Come, I'll show you, *minha linda esposa*." He clicked a few buttons on the door as they left, transforming the room into a single large prison, holding the two monsters captive.

"Incredible, sir," Richard said as the two walked down the empty halls. "When are your workers returning?"

"I gave them all a little time off when I was arrested, throwing the cops off their scent. They should be back around Thursday."

"Just in time for the grand finale?" Richard asked with a wide grin.

"Indeed, Mr. Anderson, indeed." Coleman entered a seemingly endless code, scanned his hand, and stepped back as the heavy door slid open. "There she is," Dr. Coleman whispered as they entered. "*Minha linda esposa.*"

Richard gasped and took a step back in utter terror. He thought the twins were spectacular until he saw this…this…monstrosity.

The creature paced in her cage, slashing at the bars occasionally. Her body constantly crouched under the looming ceiling. She couldn't have been less than fourteen feet, her claws as long as a shotgun, her mouth three times the size of Richard's head.

She was truly a monster.

"Wow," was all Richard could mutter.

"Isn't she beautiful?" Coleman asked as he admired her.

Richard gathered his courage and inched close to her cage. "Mrs. Coleman, you look as lovely as ever."

"What may have seemed like a failed attempt at curing and saving my beautiful Elenor turned into my greatest accomplishment. An unstoppable beast," the doctor sighed contently.

"Have you named your species yet, sir?"

Coleman wrapped his hand around the bar, his eyes shining. "Rifkins."

The Rifkin opened her arms and let out an ear-splitting roar, shaking the entire room. Richard covered his ears and screamed with her to block out the noise, but it was a lost cause.

When she stopped, Richard let go of his ears. His hands were spotted with blood. "My ears," he cried, yelling deafly. "They won't stop ringing!"

Coleman seemed unfazed as he started walking out. "Tinnitus, drink some celery juice and you'll be fine."

Richard opened his mouth to try and pop his aching ears. "Does it ever go away?"

Coleman laughed, almost hysterically. "If it does, let me know."

CHAPTER 22

Matt buried his face in his hands, hating the feeling of tears soaking his palms. The scene was all too familiar. Cops raiding his living room, detectives pounding his mom for any answers, a hollow feeling in the messy house. The only difference was the subject of the cause.

"Matt," the chief whispered quietly.

Matt forced himself to sit up and wiped his nose across his arm.

"We gotta stop hanging out so much, dude," he tried to joke. When Matt didn't respond, he sighed and put his hand on the boy's shoulder. "Please talk to me, son."

Matt jumped out of the couch and glared at the chief. "I just got my sister back, and now my younger siblings are gone! What am I supposed to say? Huh? 'Don't worry, they're probably fine back at the lab with—'" He stopped suddenly and swore. "Oh my gosh! Oh my—"

"What's up?" the chief asked inquisitively.

"Where's Drew?" His heart was pounding so hard he could feel it in his neck. "Where's Detective Phillips?"

The chief furrowed his brow. "He's doing the perimeter. Matt, what's going on?"

Matt didn't waste another second. "I have to go. I'll explain everything later!" He sprinted out the door and around the house until he practically tackled Drew.

"Woah, easy there ti—" He stopped and gave a pitiful smile. "Oh, hey, Matt, how ya doing?"

Matt pushed down his true feelings and launched right into it. "The Minefield, Drew! Coleman spent the last years of his wife's life creating the Minefield, right? But instead of it curing her, it turned her into a...angry huge beast, considering the first Minefield subject and serum an utter failure."

"Well, yeah, that's what Hope and Harmony were telling us but—"

Matt began to pace around Drew as he talked, growing more passionate by the second. "But what if he didn't consider that failure? What if that's what he meant to do?"

"What do you mean?"

"Do you still have Coleman's notebooks?"

Drew reached into his satchel and pulled out the faded red book, handing it to him without a second thought.

Matt flipped through the pages quickly. "I was studying these while you were with the Coleman girls, and I found...this!" He held up the book for Drew to see.

Drew looked at the paper, back at Matt, and shrugged. "Still gibberish, my guy."

Matt resisted the urge to be frustrated. "It says here, 'With the expected dosage of Minefield subject no. 1, there is enough remaining for two additional subjects.'"

"Matt," Drew said breathlessly, "what are you saying?"

"I'm saying I think I know why Coleman took Taylor and Tyler." Matt looked back at the house, where the chief was talking to his distraught mother. "We need to leave now."

"What about—"

"I have four guns in the garage, I'm leaving now before it's too late. Are you coming?" Matt almost demanded.

Drew clenched his jaw, his options rolling around in his head. "On one condition," he argued.

"We can't take the chief, Drew. What I want to do defies his protocol."

Drew almost scoffed. "No, he'll stay here and watch over your sister and Lucas. We need to take Hope Coleman with us." Matt scoffed in surprise. "A-are you joking? We can't take his *daughter*."

"And why's that?" said a feminine voice from behind Matt. "You think I can't handle myself against the esteemed Dr. Cole Coleman?"

Matt turned slowly to face the girl, who was now holding a small silver pistol at his chest. "Woah," he said, putting his hands up in surrender. "That's not what I meant at all. I just mean I don't want you getting hurt or having to watch what we have to do."

Hope laughed and tucked the gun back into the waste of her pants. "Relax, kid, I've thought of nothing other than killing that piece of garbage for the past nineteen years. If anyone gets to pull the trigger and watch his blood pour, it's me."

Matt squinted. "Were you already on your way to the lab?" he asked, looking into Drew's loaded bag. "You've got enough ammo to kill an army."

Drew gave Matt a sheepish look. "Before you get mad, we were gonna invite you, but you're already one step ahead! So shall we?"

Hope batted a painted eyelash. "Lead the way, Detective Anderson. We've got kids to save and men to kill." She brushed past the boys and climbed into Matt's red truck.

Matt whistled as she shut the door.

Drew shook his head. "Don't get any ideas, Matthew. That is the girl of my dreams."

Matt blinked. "Oh, go for it, she scares me."

Drew blushed and started walking toward the truck. "Me too, but as feelings dance over the contradiction of love and fear, there's nothing more terrifying or beautiful than a tough chick."

*****

Karissa

"Please," the man begged, his breaths raspy. "It hurts."

"Poor little guy," the cynical voice slithered out my lips. "Whatever shall we do?" I raised my foot and slammed the heel onto his already crushed fingers.

He screamed as I began twisting my foot in a circle. "Stop!"

In an instant, I pulled him to his feet and held him inches away from my face. "You think you get to tell me what to do?"

"N-no."

"That's right," I growled. "Nobody gets to tell Sienna what to do."

The man glanced at Dr. Coleman. "Not even him?"

Rage filled every available part of my body. I ignored Coleman's "torture, but don't kill. I'd like to speak with him" order and dug my fingers into the back of his neck. Without a second thought, I threw him against the concrete as hard as I could. His body splattered on the ground, making a sickening noise as he died.

"Sienna!" Coleman scolded, his voice echoing in my head. "I specifically told you not to kill him!"

I sneered at the man who had controlled me for the past two years. "Nobody tells Sienna what to do."

Coleman pulled me toward him by the hair, holding the Punisher to my neck. "Is that what you think? You think you get to be the boss now?"

"I could kill you in an instant if I wanted to," I shot back, venom hanging on every word.

"Ha!" Coleman said, spitting in my face. "Think again, sweetheart." He clicked on the Punisher, shooting sharp electric pains straight down my spine. "I own you."

*****

My eyes flew open.

It couldn't have been later than 3:00 a.m. I was sitting up in Lucas's bed, with him lying peacefully beside me. The room was silent, only lit by the pale full moon shining through the dirty window. Lucas let out a sigh; luckily, I hadn't woken him. His hair was wild, his bare chest covered in goosebumps, just like the day I had taken him.

Oh my gosh.

I ran to the bathroom and shut the door as quickly and quietly as I could. My head was drenched in my sweat. I couldn't seem to catch my breath. Everything felt like it was moving at hyperspeed, yet nothing was happening.

The girl in the mirror stared back at me, just as terrified as the memories came flying back.

Blood, terror, suffering, pain, screaming, crying, sobbing, death, all caused by *me*. With each tick of the clock, I remembered each and every second of the last two years. I remembered every drop of blood I had spilled.

The lady in the restaurant was right, I was a merciless murderer who didn't deserve to live. My chest felt hollow as I silently sobbed over the sink, overcome by what I had done.

During the lonely nights in the lab, where remorse should have set in, instead, I craved more power from Dr. Coleman.

Oh my gosh.

Dr. Coleman.

He was the man who had saved me the night of the date. No. *He* was the one who kidnapped me the night of the date. *He* was the one who orchestrated the whole fight. *He* was the one who injected me with the ability to kill without sympathy, without any guilt. *He* was the one who had spent nineteen years stalking me for my genetics.

Every loss, every ounce of anguish, every drop of unearned blood was all his fault.

But I wasn't innocent.

I was the one who had actually done all of it. All he did was pull the strings while I did the work.

While I did the killings.

Outside the door, Lucas's phone rang.

I suddenly realized I was on the ground, holding my knees while tears freely fell down my cheeks. There wasn't a single part of my body that wasn't trembling. I felt like a child.

Lucas knocked on the door lightly. "Karissa? Are you in here?"

I didn't answer. Maybe if I tried hard enough, I could disappear completely.

"Karissa, can I come in?"

Lucas had given up his entire life for me, a murderer, a merciless serial killer. I didn't deserve his love. I didn't deserve to live.

He pushed the door open a few inches. "Hey, cute girl, you oka—" I watched his features fall as he caught sight of me, folded and broken on the bathroom floor. "Hey, hey, hey, what's up?" Without a second thought, he sat cross-legged next to me, wrapping his strong arms around my shivering shoulders.

"Lucas," I whispered, even my voice sounding weak. "I did it all."

He didn't react, just watched me carefully, waiting for me to go on.

"That lady was right. I am an inhuman murderer who doesn't deserve to live." I sobbed.

Lucas lifted me into his lap, cradling me like a child, still not uttering a word.

"I remember everything," I blubbered.

"It wasn't your fault," he whispered, his voice shaking. "You have to understand it wasn't your fault."

His words only made me confirm I didn't deserve him. I had just told him I remember every person I killed, and he continued to defend me.

"I could've stopped him, Lucas. I could've stopped him at any point, and I didn't."

"You tried, Karissa, you tried." He put his hand on my cheek, letting my head rest against his chest. "I watched you fight against his decisions for months, and each time, you would come back with less control and more Minefield in your eyes."

"I could've done more." I wept.

Lucas sat up, forcing me to look at him and his sorrowful face. "It's important to me that you know I 100 percent know there is no blood on your hands. There is no reason for you to feel guilt. However, I also know there isn't one thing I could say to make you feel better."

I took a shaky breath, hiccuping on more sobs.

"So now here's what I'm going to tell you. Karissa, you survived two years with the most corrupt man on this earth. You are not your past because your past betrayed you. You are not a bad person. You are not evil. You aren't just a fighter. You are a hero. You are here, right now, with the power to shape today, tomorrow, and the rest of your life." His voice grew with each word, filling me and him with pure passion. "You are Karissa Anderson, the most beautiful, kind, perfect girl I've ever known. No matter what happened, what is happening, or what may happen, I've loved you forever, and I'll love you always."

For a second, I was positive my heart stopped. Lucas Carter told me he loved me, *the Lucas Carter* had told me he loved me. The boy I had spent seventeen years living and breathing for even a glance in my direction. The high school crush I stayed up all night long waiting for a text back. The man that had given up his entire life to saving me. Lucas Carter had just told me he loved me even though I wasn't worth a single syllable of those precious three words. "Lucas, I—"

He picked up my hand and kissed the top of it. "And don't you think for a second you don't deserve it. I would give up everything for you, Karissa. I would do literally anything for you. I love you, Swan Lake."

I put my hand on his chest, feeling his fragile beating heart kiss my fingers. "Lucas, I've loved you forever."

His sorrowful features cracked, and a full smile spread across his cheeks. His perfect dimples poked through his jaw. Lucas was beautiful; he was so handsome. How lucky was I that he was here with me forever?

I sat up, inches away from him, feeling as if gravity was pulling me like a magnet. He closed his eyes. I held my breath. My hand was on his bare chest. His fingers were in my hair.

His body tensed.

Chills waved over me.

We were a moment apart.

Finally, the world felt right.

Lucas's lips met mine with such force and beauty I thought nothing else would feel as perfect as him. He pulled me as close as possible until there wasn't a breath of air between us. I melted into his arms, flooding with pure relief.

At that moment, I understood why wars were fought and minds were lost over love. I would do anything for Lucas. Euphoria filled my veins as his hands wrapped around my waist, making me feel completely and wholly protected from whatever this life had to throw at me.

My lips moved with his, a smile creeping onto my face as our kisses deepened. My hands wandered up to his hair until my arms were wrapped around his head.

Lucas pulled me closer, pushing his face into my stomach, sudden sobs overwhelming him. His entire body shook as each wail escaped his lips.

I refused to let him go. I laid my head on top of his, my arms still holding his neck. "Lucas? What's wrong?"

He couldn't get control. His howls broke my heart.

The more he cried, the more scared I got. "Lucas, who called you?"

His fingers moved back to my waist. He pried himself off my stomach, now soaked with his tears, and looked me deep in the eyes. "Karissa…"

I reclaimed my place on the floor beside him, wiping his tears with my thumbs. "Lucas?"

"Karissa, Coleman has your siblings."

CHAPTER 23

Matt peered through the scope of the gun, his finger hovering over the safety. "Coleman Labs, where we believe in one door and half a window," he said in Coleman's announcing voice.

Hope snorted and continued shoving bullets into her pistol. "So, Matt, tell me about yourself. How'd you get all roped into this? Are you a cop?"

Matt sat back below the grass, joining Drew and Hope. "Karissa, uh, Sienna is my sister. That's all."

Drew nudged Matt. "Don't let him fool you. Matt was the reason we got Karissa out of there, and he saved Detective Carter's life."

Hope raised her eyebrows, impressed. "Well, look at you go. And where is Detective Carter these days?"

"He's with Karissa, trying to get her adjusted to…everything," Matt explained. "Like the other night, this crazy lady tried to kill her, screaming about how Sienna killed her cousin or something."

Hope swore, shaking her head in disgust. "My father's done a lot of horrible things, but he was right about one thing. Growing up, he always told us that as humans, the overpowering species of the world, it would be so easy to create Utopia. Instead, we spend our short lives tearing each other apart."

Drew looked up at the cloudy sky, threatening to rain. "If Minefield would have gone differently, I could see the purpose. Minus the unwilling torturing of a teenager. Done right, Coleman really could've changed the world."

Hope cracked her knuckles, her glare practically burning through the air as she stared at the compound. "I will get revenge for your sister, Matt."

"So," Drew said after a long minute of absolute silence, "how many kids do you have, Hope?"

She turned her Earth-burning glare and directed it at Drew. "Excuse you?"

He paled. "At your house...I, uh, all those kids, I—"

"Relax," she said, breaking into a grin. "I knew what you meant. I just wanted to see you sweat." She sighed and leaned back. "My sister hooked up with this guy right after our parents left. He was some doofus full of money and lies."

The boys shared a glance, not knowing what to say.

"Five kids one right after the other, and, bam, he disappeared," she spat angrily.

"So your sis—"

The entire ground shook as a deafening roar echoed from the lab.

Hope flinched, pulling the trigger on her gun. The sudden noise made the three of them jump to their feet in surprise.

Drew looked toward the compound, fear filling his soul. "What was that?"

Matt slung his gun over his shoulder. "Whatever it was, it must have heard your gun. We need to get out of here."

Hope snorted. "Are you joking? We came here to kill Coleman—"

"And get the twins," Drew added.

She sighed. "We came here to kill Coleman, and get the twins, and that's exactly what I'm gonna do."

Matt tapped his foot anxiously. "No, we'll come back with the element of surprise still on our hands. We're sitting ducks if they heard us."

"Matt's right," Drew urged. "We'll come back more prepared."

"No," Hope argued, still holding tight to her gun. "I'm not leaving until I get revenge on my father for what he did to me, my sister, and Karissa!" she shouted.

"Drew..." Matt said quietly, pointing over the tall grass.

Drew looked toward the lab and gasped. "We really gotta go, now!"

Hope continued to argue, but Drew's instincts took over. He started running, throwing Hope over his shoulder as they sprinted. Matt gathered the rest of the abandoned supplies and ran with them.

As Hope bounced up and down on Drew's sharp shoulder blade, she saw the guards chasing after them. "Faster!" she cried.

Matt dug his keys out of his pocket as fast as he possibly could. He slammed his fingers on the little buttons and cursed as the panic alarm started ringing. "Get in! It's unlocked!"

"Matt, the alarm!" Drew yelled back, throwing his gun into the bed of the truck.

"Yeah, don't worry, Drew, I hear it!" Matt retorted, sling-shotting himself into the driver's seat. He slashed his seat belt across his chest and looked back at Drew and Hope.

Drew launched into the back seat, with Hope still tangled behind him. Matt turned the key and slammed it into gear, peeling out of the tall dry grass.

Hope squealed as a bullet shattered the back window. Drew shoved her head down, covering her with one arm while firing back with the other.

Matt drifted around the trees, spinning the wheel in all different directions as the truck spun on two tires. His years of doing doughnuts in the dance studio's parking lot were about to pay off.

"Hey! We're losing 'em!" Drew shouted excitedly. "Nice driving, tex!"

An explosion hit the back of the truck, sending the vehicle flying into the air. Once the truck was airborne, the flipping began. The ground was moving so many times that Matt lost track of which way was up. His body slammed against his seat belt until the force of his body ripped it off. His head smashed into the steering wheel. Matt could practically feel his brain ramming against his skull.

Drew slid into the window, holding onto the door handle with all his strength. His torso whipped around him as he held tight. He watched Hope's body bounce off the roof then back to the ground then to the seat. In a single desperate heroic act, he opened an arm and caught her, hanging on to her abdomen while the truck rolled to a stop.

The kids didn't even have a chance to take a breath before the doors were ripped off by the guards. They seized the kids by their bloody broken arms and dragged them out.

Matt groaned, his stomach threatening to turn over as the guard pulled him to his feet. "See, Johnson? I told you they wouldn't give us any trouble."

"Oh, I don't feel good," Matt mumbled, his legs shaking.

The guard tossed him over his shoulder, threatening even more nausea for Matt.

"Supposedly, they were the ones that took down Admiral Coleman and kidnapped Sienna," the guard holding Drew shrugged.

"Well, well, well, what do we have here?" the third guard smirked, yanking Hope to her feet. "Ms. Coleman? It's good to see you, my dear."

She glared, a look that could kill.

"Admiral will be excited with what we've found. We should get them back before he sends the Rifkins after us."

That got a chuckle out of the whole group.

As the kids were hauled back toward the compound, Drew knew it was now or never. If they were taken to the lab, there was a small chance all three of them would get out. He couldn't take that chance, not after how far they'd come.

Drew stumbled on a rock and belly-flopped to the ground, catching himself with the tips of his fingers.

"Up. Now," his captivator demanded.

Filling his lungs with as much air as they would take, Drew propped himself on his elbows, sweeping his foot under the guard's legs. The man toppled, giving Drew seconds to sling his gun out of his holster.

The two others stopped in their tracks, aiming their weapons at Drew. Drew didn't falter. He held his ground, pointing the barrel of the gun right at the man's nose.

The guard swallowed hard and raised his arms in surrender. "Well, aren't you a hero?"

Drew loaded the gun and motioned toward the other two. "You tell them to drop my friends, now."

"Whatcha gonna do? Kill me?" He laughed. "Mercy compared to being a traitor to Admiral Coleman."

"If you don't," Drew pushed, "I'll make you feel pain you can't even imagine."

"Son," he scoffed, "I already have."

Drew's ears perked as he heard a leaf crunch behind him. He flew around to see Matt's guard sneaking toward him. Drew, without a single thought otherwise, fired the gun, straight between his collarbones. The man gasped and collapsed, dying in seconds. Matt fell unconscious beside his body.

He lowered the gun and fired at his guard, blowing a perfect hole straight through his forehead.

"Drew," Hope squeaked.

Drew kept his hand tight on his weapon even as his courage began shaking. Hope winced under the barrel of the gun her guard shoved against her temple. "Drop the gun," he ordered.

"Fine," Drew whispered, carefully laying his gun on the edge of his toe and raising his hands in surrender. "Let her go."

He loaded the gun, grinning with joy as he did. "Why should I? This is the famous Hope Coleman, is it not?" He slid his fingers around her waist. "I've heard she's a firecracker."

That did it.

Drew flicked his foot, flinging the gun perfectly into his palm. He lowered his aim and fired right at the man's hand, knocking his gun out of his obliterated fingers. Drew fired again, right into his stomach, knocking him down in an instant.

Hope watched him fall and high-fived Drew as he crouched beside him.

"You think you're the hotshot hero," the man pushed, his teeth stained red with his blood. "But we were the first of *thousands* sent to get you."

Hope stood over Drew's shoulder. "What's that supposed to mean?"

"It means," he stopped to grunt, his organs beginning to seep out of his bullet wound, "it's already too late for Sienna and her detective. It means you're already dead."

Drew stood, his body flooding with adrenaline. "My, I…the phone, I—"

Behind them, a wave of armed guards was roaring toward them.

Hope snatched the gun out of Drew's hand and fired, killing the last man instantly. "Go get them, Drew."

He put his hand on her back, leading her away from the lab. "Yeah, let's get Matt and—"

She stopped and pushed his hand off. "No, Drew. We don't have time. Go get them."

"You can't be serious, Hope." His eyes welled with tears. "I'm not leaving without you or Matt."

She cracked her neck. "Yes, you are. If we don't stop my dad in time, he'll kill us and everyone we know. At least this way we have a chance!"

He clenched his jaw as he fought more tears, his opinion not swayed. "I'm not leaving you to die."

She grunted in frustration. "You're not! We're using me and Matt as a diversion! He'll be so distracted by the fact his sweet daughter came to see him. I'll convince him not to hurt Matt long enough for you to bring some backup and make sure Karissa and Lucas are safe. Got it?"

"Hope, I can't just—"

"Leave right now or I swear I'll scream Lucas's address," she half-joked, shoving him away.

Drew took one last look at the massacre around him. Hope gave an encouraging nod, glancing at Matt still lying face down. "I swear, I'll get us out of this."

She smiled genuinely for the first time since Drew had met her, and by goodness, it was the most beautiful sight he'd ever seen.

He would do anything to see her smile again.

His life no longer belonged to him, it belonged to Hope and his own faltering hope.

CHAPTER 24

Karissa

Lucas's hand seemed to be the only thing keeping me pinned to reality as we stepped over the police line. He looked around at the cop cars lining the street, a hollow look in his eyes.

Maybe this scene was all too familiar.

I hesitated as I stared into the small kitchen.

"You okay?" Lucas asked.

I held his gaze, my smile shaking as I forced it to spread across my cheeks. "My mom still thinks I'm Sienna, and the last time I saw Matt, I tried to kill him."

Lucas took a long breath in. "Your mom will see you and know it's you, not Sienna. You just have to have faith in her."

"And Matt?"

"And Matt," Lucas swallowed, having a hard time keeping himself collected, "risked his life to save you at the lab."

My attention switched to the crooked frames hanging on the walls. "If Coleman touches one hair on the twin's heads, I'll go full Sienna and tear him apart."

"Well, well, well," the chief greeted, his booming voice bouncing. "By the stars, Karissa Anderson, the lost princess, is finally home!" He opened his arms, the first person, besides Lucas, not afraid of my touch.

I wrapped myself in his tight hug and let out a chuckle. "Sir, I'd like to thank you for all you've done for me and my family."

He released me, keeping his big hands tight on my shoulders. His powerful eyes were dotted with emotion. "I love ya like I'd love a daughter. I'd do anything for you and your family." He sniffed and in an instant regained his chiefly appearance. "Which leads me to the subject at hand. I've got a team working around the clock to get all the information we can."

Lucas put his hand on my back, making me relax in an instant. "Anything I can do, Chief?"

"Just keep doing what you're doing, Carter," he said with a wink and nod. "Now that Coleman's out, keeping Ms. Anderson safe and away from him is crucial." The chief took a breath. "There's someone who'd like to meet you, Karissa."

While Lucas walked around the house, greeting other cops and detectives, I followed the chief across my forgotten house.

A woman with soft features and worn eyes stood as we made our way into the dining room. "Karissa." She threw her arms around me, her body shuddering with her shallow breaths. "It's nice to meet you."

I nervously chuckled and released the hug. "Thank you…and you are?"

She shook her head and laughed with me. "I'm Harmony, Harmony…Coleman."

The name sent a dark chill spinning down my spine. My smile fell. "I'm sorry? Did you say…Coleman?" I wanted Lucas to hold me back to reality; I needed him.

"I just wanted to, uh, apologize, on my father's account," she said, her bright eyes wandering around the room. "I know it won't count for anything, but it's important to me that you know."

My tense shoulders relaxed as she spoke. "Oh," I said lamely. "Well, it means a lot. Thank you. Seriously." Her smile grew, and she nodded enthusiastically.

"My sister, Hope, feels the same. I'm sure she'd love to meet you too." She clicked her tongue as she scanned the house. "That's weird."

"What's up?"

"She was just here."

HITTING THE GROUND RUNNING

The world tilted around me. Something was wrong, I could feel it.

The chief lowered his phone and whispered something to Lucas, who stood beside him. Lucas clenched his jaw, his eyes hollow yet rageful.

Matthew.

Where was Matt?

Drew.

Where was Drew?

Hope.

Where was Hope?

A hand grabbed my shoulder, turning me aggressively. I turned and everything changed.

I wasn't in the house anymore. I wasn't safe anymore.

I was in the lab.

Coleman's hand held tight to me, his sardonic grin slowly inching up his jaw. "Karissa."

My hands wrapped around his, but I couldn't pull him off. "No. Stop! You're not real. This isn't real."

"*This* may not be real. But *this*," he opened his arms and gestured out, "is."

"No!" I screamed.

Matt lay on the concrete floor, beaten and thrashing in pain. He stretched his hand out, my name echoing off his lips. The scene was all too familiar.

Coleman circled me, his hot breath bouncing off my neck. "This is all your fault, Karissa. Look at all the pain and misery you've caused. Look what you've done to your brother. How dare you?"

"Matt!" I cried. My scars burned, my eyes pulsed, and power ripped its way down my arms. At that moment, I felt like I could do anything. I knew, if pushed hard enough, I could rip Coleman's head off without breaking a sweat.

"Yes!" Coleman cheered, making me jump. "I knew Sienna wasn't gone! I knew she was buried under that coward."

I looked at my hands, hands that could kill, and wrapped them around my waist. "Sienna's gone," I spat, disgust drowning each word. The power evaporated. My scars resumed their dull color. I was right, Sienna couldn't come out unless I let her.

Coleman pulled me toward him, his fingers locked around my hair. His face was an inch away. With each word, he got closer, and the power he had over me was evident. "Say what you will, sweetheart, but no matter what, I will be there just like before. I will be watching you, infesting your life. My final plan is perfected, Karissa, and you will die. Along with Lucas, Matt, Taylor, Tyler, Drew, and anyone else you've ever known." He yanked me closer and planted a single kiss on my lips. "I'll see you tonight, my dear."

In an instant, I was back in the house, staring at the ceiling. Blurry images focused into people hovering over me, their faces traced with concern. My chest was filled with air I couldn't release. I wanted to scream, maybe I already was. All my senses were gone.

Until Lucas's hand landed on my cheek, bringing me back to reality.

The awful, true, horrible reality.

"Karissa?" he asked quietly. "Can you hear me?"

I forced myself to sit up, avoiding everyone else's eye contact. "Coleman—" I spurted, still yelling.

"What about him?" the chief said. "What did you see, Karissa?"

Lucas kept his hand on my cheek, forcing me to focus solely on him. "Sweetie, what did you see? What did Coleman say?"

I took three shaky breaths before closing my eyes and trying to put it all into words. "He has Matt. He's coming. He's coming tonight. He's going to kill everyone I love. He's going to kill me."

"It's all your fault," a new voice declared.

All attention switched to her, my mom. She stood in front of us, her arms crossed, her gaze dead. She was numb, not a single emotion left in her heart. "Kathrine…" the chief whispered in disbelief.

"Mom," I mumbled.

She didn't stand down. "If you had died two years ago like we thought, none of this would be happening. The twins would be safe. Matt would be happy. Lucas would have a life. This is all your fault."

Lucas's concerned demeanor switched to shocked anger. "Excuse me?"

"Get out of my house before you ruin another life."

The chief stood, his hands resting on his belt, trying to appear casual. "Ya know what, Kathrine, why don't we have a chat in the kitchen?"

A fake smile plastered on her face. "Sure thing, I just need to say goodbye to *Sienna* one last time."

Lucas pulled me to my feet but still stood in front of me, protecting me from my own mother.

The look on her face would've made Coleman proud. "When you get to hell, be sure to tell Richard hello." And with that, she patted my forehead, spun on her heel, and walked out of my life forever.

The chief watched her saunter away and shook his head. "Carter, get Ms. Anderson home, now. We have to assume Coleman is coming tonight in full arms. Lock all doors, windows, doggy gates, I don't care what it is, lock it up. Keep your gun close and Karissa closer."

Lucas gave a single nod. "Yes, sir."

"Harmony, come with me to the station, we need to get in contact with your sister."

Harmony put a hand on her chest. "You don't think she's working with him, do you?"

"We have to assume the worst with Coleman. But I'll do everything in my power to get her, the boys, and the twins out of his grasp," he promised. "I will do what it takes to put a bullet in his heart."

The chief was right.

Coleman needed to die.

And I was the only one who could kill him.

CHAPTER 25

*B*ang.

It was a cliché movie scene. I bolted up in bed, my hair wild, drenched in sweat, gasping for air. My latest nightmare sat fresh on the tip of my mind. I slowly laid back in Lucas's bed, pulling the blanket up to my chin.

The curtains danced in the wind, giving a perfect view of the open window. The breeze circled the room, giving an eerie feeling. In a fit of panic, I twisted around, reaching for Lucas. My hand fell through where his body was supposed to be. His spot was still warm. I bolted up before I could tell my brain to do anything else.

"Lucas?" I whisper-shouted.

The breeze from the window creaked the bathroom door open. The light was off.

As quietly as possible, I pulled the nightstand drawer open and wrapped my fingers around Lucas's gun. I crept forward, keeping the gun aimed at the ground.

I had to remind myself who I was.

I was the most feared weapon in the world. I was genetically enhanced to kill.

There was nothing I couldn't do.

With a single grunt, I kicked the door open, aiming the gun at every inch of the bathroom.

Nothing.

Nothing except the tiny window, wide open, blowing more air in.

"Lucas!" I called, my voice growing with urgency. "Lucas!" My heart pounded as I sprinted out of the room, throwing the door to the stairwell off its hinges.

My scars burned, my eyes pulsed, and power ripped its way down my arms. At that moment, I believed I could do it all. I could use Sienna's powers for myself.

I reached the lobby floor with nothing but a gun, pajamas, and a scrunchie.

The stunning lobby looked eerie in the light of the pale moon.

Each piece of furniture looked ready to pounce.

The shadows from the bar could hide anything.

My bare feet tingled, every nerve in my body alive and ready.

A grandfather clock in the corner burst into song as the hour hand hit two. I jumped and fired, hitting the clock through its face. The cheerful song became a haunting lullaby as it died.

"Isn't music strange?"

I spun, my gun still smoking.

Lucas sat on the grand piano's bench, gently pressing one key at a time. "We stretch our vocal cords, and suddenly, it's more than words. It's a feeling. With just a simple action, we can create our own symphony."

I lowered the gun and knelt by his side, my hands still shaking. "Lucas? What are you doing down here?"

He pressed another key and smiled. His hair was perfect, his beard freshly shaven. A new suit replaced his usual gym shorts and no shirt bedtime look. "You know in the world we had to grow up in, it seems as though everyone was looking for a reason for a revolution."

"Lucas," I said, putting my hand on his leg. "Please, you're scaring me. What are you doing here?"

He played a simple minor melody, never looking up from his permanent stare on the instrument. "We grew up idolizing all these books, movies, and TV shows that romanticized war. Anything that would itch the craving that's been inside us since the very beginning."

These weren't Lucas's words…these were Coleman's. I gripped his leg, preparing myself for anything. The loaded gun sat against my hip.

"From the creation of man, it's been good versus evil, heaven versus hell, country versus country, right versus wrong, man versus man. It's an instinct to fight back, to fight against morality." His fingers stretched across the piano, romanticizing the melody he was playing.

"Look at me, Lucas," I said harshly, forcing my trembling voice to be confident.

He pushed the pedals, making his song echo louder in the empty lobby. "We have an urgency to fight yet we sit there complaining. If we want the world to change so badly, why isn't anyone getting up to do anything about it?"

He was practically screaming. The heat from his rage emitted off him. Yet he continued to play, smashing down on the keys as he did. I gripped his leg harder, my fingernails digging into his skin. "Look at me, Lucas. Stop playing and look at me."

"Every hour, every minute, every second, we grow lazier and stop fighting for good to even stand a chance." Sweat dripped from his nose as he kept screaming and playing. "Yet we still complain and moan about nothing changing! How can anything change if no one is doing anything? How can you be embedded with the instinct to fight back, to have 'good' win, to 'change the world for the better' and still do nothing? How?"

I shook my head as he waited for my response. "I-I don't know."

"Because the only thing that can change the world, have good win, or even have a chance at fighting back is love. And love, sweetheart, takes sacrifice. That's all it is." He raised his face, confirming my worst fear. His perfect green eyes were now infected with the Minefield's red. "So let me ask you something. Are you willing to sacrifice everything for love?"

My hands planted themselves on his cold cheeks. "Lucas, you have to listen to me. Fight this. You can do it. You can push the thoughts away."

He put his own hands over my wrists, gripping them tightly. "You didn't answer me. Are you willing to sacrifice everything for love?"

"Push the thoughts down, Lucas," I cried. "Push back. Fight it."

He cocked his head and started to stand. "I need an answer," he roared, fury sinking into every word. "If you are who you say you are, you're done being Sienna, you're really done killing, that means you, too, have the urge to fight for good. You believe you have enough love inside your miserable broken heart to save your family, your friends, to save me. Is that right?" His grasp on my wrist was growing tenser as if he was ready to snap the bones at any second.

"Yes," I whispered, pleading in my eyes. "That's right."

"Good." His hands moved from my wrists to my neck in a flash. His lips curled into a gruesome sneer.

I took one last breath and dropped the gun. "Let Lucas go, Coleman," I rasped. "Let him go."

He laughed. "You're Sienna. You have the power to rip an entire army apart limb by limb. And instead, you've been spending the last few weeks being publicly humiliated by an angry soccer mom in a diner."

My eyes locked with what used to be my Lucas's. I knew he was still in there.

"You could spend the rest of your life devoting every living breathing second to making up for what you've done and still not deserve this boy," a rich voice said, his words bouncing through my head.

A single tear slipped down my cheek.

Coleman emerged from the darkness, standing an inch behind Lucas. "My dear sweet Sienna, what have you become?" He wiggled the tablet controlling Lucas tauntingly.

The sight of him pushed every ounce of anger I had to the surface. "Lucas did nothing to you. Let him go," I said between my last gulps of air.

"Wrong!" Coleman announced. "When I told Mr. Carter he would pay with his own blood for making you weak, he said, 'If that's what it takes.' Lucas deserves to be hurt just as much as you do."

Stars danced in front of my eyes, but I refused to die like this. I refused to leave Lucas in the hands of Coleman.

"One single button and I could stop pretty boy's heart."

This had to end.

Coleman had to die.

And I was the only one who could kill him.

I closed my eyes, letting Sienna's power flood my veins. I groaned as my muscles contorted to her liking. My head pounded. My scars burned. My joints cracked.

There she was.

Coleman bit back his grin as I opened my eyes, letting my anger take over. I wrapped my clawlike fingers around Lucas's arms and pried them off my neck, leaving bruises on his skin.

Lucas pulled himself out of my grasp and picked me up by the shirt, trying to throw me.

I flipped over his head, bringing him crashing to the ground in the process.

It was Coleman's turn.

I snarled and lunged at him, throwing my leg around his middle and hanging onto his back. My hands went to the tablet, prying it out of his greedy little hands.

I looked at the options on the screen: **Attack**, **Defend**, **Kill**, **Self-Destruct**.

Within those buttons were thousands of other commands.

But the one that caught my eye was one simple button: **Release**.

I clicked it.

Lucas groaned and collapsed, his eyes wide as the Minefield left his eyes. His body thrashed and contorted before going still.

With Coleman's fingers still in the crook of my arm, I twisted each one until I heard them snap as he wailed. I was ready to pull each one out of the socket until they were ripped out of his palm, but he broke out in laughter, making me hesitate.

"There she is!" he roared, his haunting cackle tickling through his words. "There's the merciless Sienna I know!"

I pulled him back by his short hair, yanking his neck back as far as it would stretch. "I'm going to kill you," I whispered, my lips brushing his ear, "and I'm going to enjoy it."

He laughed again, then thrust his elbow into the bridge of my nose. I recoiled but hung on to my hold on him. He threw it again, jabbing my temple this time. A gash stretched open. Blood gushed down my face.

My arm snaked around his head, holding his neck tightly against my elbow. "You broke my nose," I growled, feeling the warm blood trickle down my chin. "How dare you?" I pulled my grip on his neck, cutting off his supply of blood and air.

As carefully as possible, Coleman raised his fingers to his lips and let out a sharp whistle.

The lobby's stained glass windows shattered as three of his guards swung through. I tucked my head down, protecting myself from a shower of glass raining down on us. Coleman took my brief distraction to his advantage, throwing his body forward, and landing on top of me in a clumsy front flip. Before he could fully stand, I tackled him like a quarterback. I wrapped my legs over his and used one hand to hold his hands hostage. I had finally trapped him.

Without an ounce of hesitation, I punched him. Over and over again, I threw my fist into his evil broken face. With each blow, my hand was drenched in more blood, but I didn't stop.

He had killed thousands. He drowned me in his guilt. He took away my life. He had threatened my family. He had infected Lucas. He kidnapped the twins. He was torturing Matt.

Everything that happened was his fault.

The more I hit, the more blood splashed onto me, and the more I wanted to murder him. I let out a rageful scream, my head shaking with the volume. The noise bounced off the walls. The glasses in the bar shattered. The pictures slipped from the wall and crashed to the ground. The piano keys rattled. The floor trembled.

Six hands grabbed me and threw me off Coleman.

I rolled to a stop and slowly stood, cocking my head. The doctor's and my own blood drenched my hair and face. My tongue dragged across my lips, curling at the metallic taste. "Took ya long enough."

They shared a look and sprinted toward me.

The first one raised his gun, ready to fire at any moment. I took my opportunity and rolled over his back in a flash, throwing my feet into the second. The third fired his gun.

I caught the bullet, a dart filled with a thick blue serum, and laughed. "Nice shootin', tex."

He backed up, dropping his gun. "*Please*," he whispered.

My clawlike fingers snagged his shirt, dragging him face-to-face with me. "Please? Do you know how many times I said 'please' in the lab? Do you know how many times you took mercy on me?"

He looked at his toes, barely brushing the ground. "I'm sorry," he croaked.

I laughed, my teeth stained with blood. "I'm sure you are. But that doesn't change the fact that you tortured, humiliated, and destroyed me. Does it?"

He shook his head. "No."

"No, it doesn't."

His face scrunched, like a child, as he fought his tears. "I'm sorry," he cried again.

I moved my hands from his shirt to his neck, feeling each little fragile piece of bone under his skin. "I know, and that's why I'm going to kill you."

"No!" he wailed.

Just as my grip tightened, ready to shatter the life out of him, I felt a gentle hand touch the tip of my shoulder. "What?" I snapped. I threw my head around to see Lucas, my Lucas, standing beside me.

"Karissa."

The look on his face shattered my heart. A mixture of disappointment and fear. In pure shock and realization, I released my hold on the poor man, dropping him to the ground. My hands, my life-taking hands, went to my face as I began drowning in sobs.

Lucas's hands cupped my face, his fear replaced with concern. "Hey, look at me."

I hiccuped a breath in, peeking through my fingers to see him pushing a smile through his tears. "I'm a monster," I whispered.

"My Karissa is a stubborn, graceful, passionate, talented person. She's so many beautiful things, but a monster would never be on her list." His words were rich and powerful like he had true faith in each syllable.

I lowered my hands, my tears streaking through the blood on my cheeks. "Lucas," I sniffed. "I don't deserve you or this. I don't deserve to live."

Not a breath came out of his lips before they crashed into mine. I hesitated before giving in, letting myself sink into his arms. His warmth encircled me, making me feel safe, making me feel vulnerable. He took control, his fingers in my bloody hair, my hand on his rapid beating chest, not an inch between us.

Euphoria filled my veins as his hands wrapped around my waist, sending a cascade of butterflies in my stomach. My lips moved with his, relief flooding my veins as our kisses deepened. My hands wandered up his strong back, wanting nothing more than to be in his arms for the rest of my life.

"I love you, Swan Lake," he mumbled between kisses.

"I lov—"

Ouch.

I let go of Lucas as I felt a sharp pain in my neck. My legs quivered before giving out on me completely. Lucas caught me as the floor rushed up to greet me. The ceiling was spinning, the room was so hot, and the walls were shrinking. I touched my neck, yanking a small blue dart out.

"No, no, no," Lucas urged. "Stay with me, Karissa. Talk to me!"

"Lucas," I murmured, my fingers tingling. "Run."

"I'm not leaving you, Karissa!"

Two gunshots echoed behind us.

Lucas looked up, utter bewilderment in his eyes. "Drew?"

Drew swore, kneeling beside me. "I-I was coming to warn you," he panted. "I ran as fast as I could! I was supposed to warn you before…this."

"Run," I croaked again. "Please run." It was too late to save myself, that was clear, but if Lucas could get out, maybe this would've all been worth it.

"Drew!" Lucas screamed.

My vision blurred. Drew was yanked back, and a discolored figure stabbed black liquid into his neck. Drew dropped to the ground, howling in pure agony. The figure dropped him and wrapped a white cloth around Lucas's mouth.

Lucas thrashed, doing anything to fight him off. The chemical must have been too much because, within seconds, Lucas was out cold on the lobby floor.

The figure hung over me, his blood still dripping off his face. His eyes were now blazing red. Miraculously, his wounds were healing themselves right before my eyes. His purple bruises shrunk to nothing. His gashes closed in an instant.

"Oh, Karissa, you have no idea what you've done," Coleman whispered. "You've damned them all."

CHAPTER 26

"Come on. Open your eyes. Wake up." From the tips of my hair to the end of my nails, every inch of my body ached. Chills covered my skin like a disease. The floor was stone cold. Against all instincts, I opened my heavy eyelids.

"That's it, good."

I blinked a few times, forcing my vision to clear. A single naked light bulb lit our small concrete room. Dirty air filled my lungs. "Matt?" I asked once consciousness filled my brain. "Matt?"

He smiled, a full grin stretching from ear to ear. "Hey, Kay."

Ignoring the throbbing dull ache in my body, I sat up, throwing my arms around my brother. "Matt!"

He traced my spine with his fingers, lightly crying into my shoulder. "Karissa, I'm sorry for everything. I'm sorry I never helped you with chemistry. I'm sorry for stealing your charger. I'm sorry for—"

I pried him off so I could clearly look at his face. "Matthew! You have saved my life more times than I can count. You have no reason to be sorry."

He sniffled, his messy hair brushing his eyebrows. He was everything I remembered him being; he was still a lost kid. "I'm sorry you got in trouble when the twins cut their hair."

I laughed, wiping his tears away with my thumbs. "Stop apologizing! Matt, we're here, we're saf—" Reality hit me like a smack in the face. My legs pushed me up before I told them what to do. I scanned the tiny room, my heart filling with adrenaline.

Lucas sat in the corner, holding his head in his hands.

"Matt," I asked, my voice fluttering as much as my stomach was, "where are we?"

He stood with me, holding my hand like we did as kids. "Cosmos Infinite."

I squinted, giving him a peculiar look. "The space museum?"

"Also known as Coleman Labs."

*****

For as long as Evan Daniels could remember, this had been his dream.

He had worked so hard. He'd been in the department for over thirty years as the star detective. He skipped birthdays and ball games, stayed late every night, and came early every morning trying to prove himself. Years of being nothing but a workaholic paid off the second they asked him to be chief.

His ever-so-patient wife was as excited as he was. They broke the coin jar and spent every cent on his favorite restaurant to celebrate. She told everyone, bragged to the block, and messaged her entire extended family, proving once again Evan didn't deserve the sweetest woman on the planet.

He'd been chief for ten years. Hundreds of cases were solved under his control. His units worked together perfectly. The station was always spotless.

Everything seemed to be perfect.

Until the day they got the call from Kathrine Anderson.

Richard Anderson was one of Evan's closest friends growing up. They were on the same baseball team in high school. They were roommates in their small-town college. They were groomsmen at each other's weddings. They spent Independence Day in their backyards, barbecuing for each other's families. His kids would babysit the Anderson twins almost every Thursday afternoon. The Daniels and Andersons were as close to family as it could get.

Despite Richard's sudden abandonment of his family, Evan still loved that family.

He dismissed the unit en route and shoved the newest recruit onto the scene.

Watching Kathrine sob at the wobbly dining room table shattered his heart. This family didn't need any more problems, and here he was, telling them their lives would never be the same.

The deeper he got into case twenty-eight, the more he lost faith in himself as chief. Who would've known that a single missing girl could rip the world in half?

He skipped birthdays and ball games and worked from dusk to dawn, practically living at the station, trying to bring that girl home. He was ready to quit, his detectives were sleep-deprived and overworked, and the station was overrun when finally it happened. Two young detectives, a small-town kid, and a few officers brought Ms. Anderson home.

His all-too-perfect wife dropped meals off at Lucas and Ms. Anderson's doorway, not wanting to trouble them with guests but making sure they were eating. She called Evan a hero, saying he saved not only the world but the future of two kids in love.

Everything seemed to be perfect.

Until the day they got the call from Kathrine Anderson.

The chief slammed the phone down, sudden sobs whelming his body.

"Is something wrong, sir?" his newest recruit asked as he rushed into his office.

The chief raised his bloodshot eyes to the dense officer. "Yes, Detective. I have let all four Anderson children be kidnapped. All. Four." He got out of his chair so abruptly it fell to the ground. "Meanwhile Kathrine Anderson has had a complete nervous breakdown. An ambulance just arrived at her house to take her to the hospital for a suicide watch." He choked down another sob. "And if that's not enough, Detectives Carter and Phillips and Coleman's daughter are gone as well!" With a fit of fury, he threw his *World's Best Boss* mug at the wall, huffing as it shattered. "So, yes, Detective, something is wrong."

The young boy gulped. "I-I'm sorry, sir. I didn't realize—" He stopped himself, shaking away the lost sentence. "What are we going to do?"

Trying to regain his patience, Chief Daniels closed his eyes and sighed. "What do you think I am trying to figure out?"

"Sir, I may be overstepping my bounds here, but I think I have an idea," he suggested quietly.

"What? What's your idea?" he asked as if he were talking to an overactive child.

"Well, if Detective Phillips still has his walkie-talkie on him, we just send him a quick but coded message and figure out what Coleman's up to!" he explained excitedly.

"Detective?"

"Yes, sir."

"Get out of my office."

"Yes, sir."

The chief slumped in his chair and lowered his head onto the desk, not caring about the shards of glass still lying on the floor of his office. He wanted to cry more, but his shoulder shook, whimpering with the absence of his tears.

"Trouble?" asked a silky voice from outside the door.

Chief Daniels raised his head. He slid a hand to his gun and slipped a shard of the shattered mug up his sleeve.

Richard Anderson smiled as he peered around the doorframe. "Hey, there, buddy."

The chief's breath fell out of his mouth as he jumped to his feet. "Richard."

Richard walked in, casually sliding his feet on the chief's desk as he dropped into one of the chairs. "Long time no see, my good friend."

Chief Daniels raised his gun at Richard's forehead, loading it slowly. "Where are the kids?"

"How in the world would I know where they are?" He laughed, pretending to be baffled.

"You missed a camera when you got Coleman out of prison," he replied matter-of-factly.

Richard blinked, knowing his boss would never make such a fatal mistake. He made a mental note to ask him about it later. "Well, my bad! But the kids are alive…for now."

"Don't you dare hurt those kids or I'll—"

Richard laughed again. Normally, he had the laugh that could make a room bounce with joy, but now it just sounded tainted and forced. "First of all, most of those kids are my kids. Second of all, what are you going to do? Threaten to kill me and Dr. Coleman? Already tried that, didn't you?"

The chief swallowed hard, not faltering from his aim on Richard's head. "Then why are you here?"

Richard itched his head. "Had some extra time between things, thought we could catch up."

"You should be ashamed of yourself," he growled back. "You used to be in the running for my job. You were the best detective this station's ever had. Now, look at you, disgraceful."

Richard chuckled again, popping in a piece of green gum. "That's your problem, old friend. You live in the past, hold on to too many feelings."

"So you came here to tell me my problem is caring too much? Productive time well spent." He huffed. "Why are you here? Seriously."

"Well," he casually slid a gun out of his suit pocket, "I'm supposed to take care of the last threat. Which, of course, is you."

Chief Daniels didn't so much as blink at the sight of the weapon. "So kill me."

He swung the loaded gun around his finger. "Join us, Evan. Join us and live triumphantly or die a coward hiding behind your cheap fake oak desk."

"Will you answer one question before I decide?" he pushed, already knowing exactly which he would choose.

Richard let out a dramatic sigh. "Oh, you can never be quick, can you?"

"Why'd you leave your wife and kids, Rich?"

Richard stopped fiddling with his gun and put his feet on the ground.

"I've known you since we were fourteen years old. I watched you fall in love and become a husband and a father. You loved your life. You loved your family. So please just tell me why you left on some random February day," the chief pleaded.

Richard poked his cheek with his tongue, not meeting his friend's eyes. "Evan, does this mean you choose death?"

"I guess."

"I left because…" he started. "I left because it was my only choice."

The chief narrowed his eyes. "What does that mean?"

Richard reached behind his ear and pulled a tiny white wire out. He clutched it tightly in his fist, blocking any noise from getting to it. "Evan, you have to understand I did this *for* my family."

Chief Daniels waited for a response.

"When Kathrine was six months pregnant with Matt and Karissa, she fell down the stairs. They took her to the hospital as fast as they could, but it was too late. The babies were severely injured, and Kathrine had lost too much blood," he babbled, tears involuntarily falling down his cheeks. "All three of them were going to die."

"You never told me this," he said quietly.

Richard took a long breath before continuing. "I was in the hallway, trying to accept the fact that I was about to lose everything. My beautiful wife and my two kids I didn't even get to meet were going to die." He ran a hand through his hair, still fighting all his emotions. "Then this doctor sat next to me, and he put his hand on my back. He let me cry for at least forty-five minutes before uttering a single word."

Chief Daniels lowered his gun.

"He said, 'Richard, I can save them.' And I believed him. There was so much confidence in his voice I would've believed anything he would've said." He wept. "He said, 'I have the only thing that will save them. But if I do this, I need something in return.'"

"Dr. Coleman."

Richard nodded, his gaze elsewhere. "He told me if he saved them, my newborn daughter would be subject to whatever he desired. He said she had the genetics and DNA that he had been looking for,

for decades. But there was more. He made me promise that in fourteen years, he would need me to leave everything behind and come work for him."

The chief was so baffled that he took a step back to catch himself. "And you took that deal? You sacrificed your newborn daughter that easily?"

Those words lit a fuse deep inside Richard's heart. "How could you even say that?" he yelled. "It was either 'Yes, sketchy doctor, I'll come work for you and you can *borrow* my daughter' or 'Eh, I'm good. Could you give me a minute to watch my wife and kids slowly die? Thanks!' So, yes, I took the deal to allow at least a chance of a life with my family."

"Richard, I…"

"I know," he wailed as he began pacing. "You're so sorry you misjudged me. This whole time, you thought I was the crap guy who left his four kids without a dad. But now you know. You know I made a snap judgment and sacrificed everything for them. It broke my heart every day knowing they hated me for walking out." He took a big sniff, still clutching the wire in his stiff fist. "I even wrote Kathrine a letter. I was tired of the lies, I missed my kids, and I was scared for Karissa's fate. I wanted to explain everything…but she never responded."

A beat of pure and utter silence went by before he continued, "So here I am. Fulfilling a promise I made nineteen years ago."

There it was. The confession Evan had waited for since the day Richard fell off the face of the earth. Somehow, the chief didn't feel as complete as he thought it would be. It felt more like a sneaky deal turned into a corrupt life. Coleman had officially turned his best friend against him.

"Now that you got your answers," Richard finished, his dark tone slithering back into his voice. "Let's get this over with." He slid the wire back into his ear.

"Let me call my wife first," he sighed.

Richard leaned against the desk, pressing the barrel of the gun against his temple. "One wrong move and your officers will be scraping your brains off your desk. Drop your gun."

He set the gun down and dialed the number.

"*Hey, y'all, it's Lizzy Daniels,*" her voice crackled in the recorded message. "*So sorry I missed your call, hey that rhymed. Anyway, leave me a message, and I'll get back to you hopefully as soon as I can. Thanks, love ya!*"

Evan Daniels closed his eyes to picture his bride, heartbroken she hadn't answered. "Hey, Lizzy-Lou, I just wanted you to know that I love you so much. I'm sorry I've been working a lot lately. I promise I'll make it up to you. Thanks for sticking with me. You're my perfect girl, and I hope you know your guy appreciates it all. Love ya." He whimpered as he set the phone back in the cradle.

Richard looked almost guilty as he watched the whole ordeal. "I respect you, I do, Evan. I always will. So I'll make this quick. Turn around."

He clenched his jaw. "No, I'll face my death head-on."

Richard took a step back. "You always were brave. I'll give you that." He clicked the safety off and wrapped his finger around the trigger.

The chief shook his arm, feeling the cold glass slide down his arm. The split second before the trigger was pulled, he launched the glass shard.

The piece flew perfectly, arcing around the air of the bullet as it soared.

Richard dropped the gun as the glass sliced through the side of his neck. He gasped and toppled to the ground, his hand flailing as he tried to cover the gash. Blood immediately gushed down his throat, soaking the floor in seconds.

The bullet missed the chief's heart but pierced his shoulder. He mustered a groan and knelt beside his dying friend.

"Where are the kids?"

Richard coughed, his blood splattering the chief's face. "M-my ki-kids!" he forced.

"I'm going to save them, Richard! Where are they?" he roared.

"M-maze, th-the mon…the monsters from…from the lab!" was all he could say.

Richard's blood began drenching Chief Daniels's legs as he stayed beside his friend's dying side. "Please, stay with me, Rich. I need to know where the kids are."

Richard closed his eyes, his mouth dyed red as his gore made its way up his throat. "It…it's all my…my fault."

"Richard!"

Nothing.

"Richard!"

With a ragged breath, Richard felt the pains of this world slip out of his passing body.

He was dead.

Evan Daniels stood, his slacks soiled in his friend's blood, and grabbed his gun. "Detective," he called. "Get a unit together. We're going to Coleman Labs."

CHAPTER 27

Karissa

The naked light bulb flickered, adding to my already pounding head. I closed my eyes, laying my head on Lucas's lap as he gently stroked his hands through my hair.

Hope, Coleman's second daughter, sat as close as she could beside Matt. Between blubbering sobs, she explained what her father had done to her mother. He'd created a monster of some kind. An eighteen-foot, slimy, black, killing machine.

There were two smaller monsters. Fourteen-foot, energetic, uncontrollable massive creatures.

One sat back in his cage, still "transforming" as Hope put it. He was larger than the rest of them, towering another two feet over the original.

"Matt, they were horrifying," she hiccuped. "They're going to kill us."

The heavy door hissed as it slid open, and the freezing room grew even colder.

Lucas stood, helping me to my feet. He made his way to the front of the room, standing in front of all of us, our protector.

"Welcome, welcome!" Coleman greeted us, a fleet of soldiers standing behind him, weapons ready. "It's time for the grand finale."

Hope pushed past Matt and Lucas, simple wrath plain on her face. "You've had your fun, Dad. You got to kidnap us and show us your scary monsters, but now it's time to grow up and let us go."

Coleman grinned, obvious pride filling his features. "Well, look at you, Hope. Just as confident and courageous as your mother... used to be."

She laughed mockingly. "Funny, you're a real comedian."

"My sweet Hope, with all you know, I cannot let you go. But for you, I have a much better deal." He laced his fingers together casually. "Stay with me, help me operate the finale from behind the scenes."

"And why would I do that?"

"Because," he started, throwing a girl into the room with us, "if not, I'll kill your sister."

Hope gasped in horror, throwing herself next to her unconscious sister. "Harmony!" Her eyes raised to her father, a dark feeling suddenly filling the room. "Fine," she said without another thought. "I'll come with you."

"Hope, we can't trust him!" Matt yelled.

She snapped her head back, shooting a subtle look only he could see. "Guys, this is a chance."

"Take the girls to my office," Coleman instructed his guards. He watched them leave, and suddenly, he was alone with us. He was standing alone in a room with four people that wanted nothing more than to watch him die, and he just smiled.

Cole Coleman was many things. He was a psychotic killer with the ability to eliminate any threat to him or his assets. He was a brilliant doctor, scientist, and negotiator. It seemed as though nothing stood in his way.

But deep down, he was once a child hiding from a thunderstorm. He was once a quiet boy who had fallen in love with a pretty girl. He was once a scared dad for the first time.

Cole Coleman was once a simple human.

Despite the way he had gotten to this point in his life, Cole was right. Underneath all his ideas, it was all about love, and, in his words, love takes sacrifice. Cole wasn't doing this because he was scared. No, he was doing this because we were the ultimate sacrifice.

He was doing this for love.

"In just a few moments, we'll be taking a little field trip to my very special surprise! In the meantime, say your goodbyes, trust me, you'll want to get all those last words out. Then we'll load up!" he said as if he was rallying a soccer team. "Good luck!" He winked, spun, and slammed the door shut.

For a moment, we all stood completely still, absorbing our death sentences.

Then a quiet voice from the back whispered, "How do we get out of this one?"

I turned, seeing my brother leaning against the wall, fighting back his panic. "We stick together," I said, surprising myself. "Coleman's one to play with his food. Whatever's out there is going to be some kind of 'game' for him. Don't let him get in your head."

The boys nodded.

I pulled them into a big hug, breathing in the familiar smell of my home and my Lucas. "I can't lose you guys," I cried into their shoulders. "Promise me you'll fight."

"Of course, Karissa," Lucas said, rubbing my back with the tips of his fingers.

"I promise, Kay," Matt mumbled.

I leaned back, rubbing my tears on my shoulders. "Any last words, y'all?" I chuckled tearfully.

Lucas raised his hand and smiled at Matt. "When this is all over, I want you to come work at the station."

He scoffed lightly, baffled. "I'm sorry?"

"Seriously, Matt. You've been the biggest aid in solving this case. We literally couldn't have done it without you. You have a gift," he praised. "So *when* we get out of here, promise me you'll think about it."

"Detective Anderson, eh?" he said with a grin. "I like it."

"You'll think about it?" Lucas asked excitedly.

"Heck yeah!"

I threw my arms around my brother, suddenly overwhelmed with nostalgia. "Thank you for everything, Matt."

He hugged me back, tighter. "I'm sorry, Kay."

"Stop saying that."

It was as if I was watching our childhood through a screen when I looked at his face. We had been inseparable for fourteen years. He was the person who taught me to be strong and brave. Matt wasn't afraid to let me get hurt as long as he was there to show me how to fight back. He was my live-in best friend. No matter how old we got, Matt would always be the eight-year-old with a chipped tooth, a face full of freckles hidden under a baseball cap, leading our adventures in the abandoned museum.

"Can I tell you something?" he asked, his lip quivering.

I just nodded, afraid of my emotions if I replied.

"I quit football for Mom," he said with a quiet sob. "I got a job, dealing, and paid the bills she couldn't. I paid for the dance classes for you and Taylor. I paid for football for Tyler. I'm not proud of the way I had to earn the money," he admitted, "but I am proud that I kept us in a house."

My jaw dropped. Guilt filled my heart for every argument we had over him and football. I wanted nothing more than to go back in time and hug the boy who had saved us from losing the house we grew up in.

"I'm sorry I never told you."

I brushed his tears with my thumbs and kissed his forehead, just like Mom used to. "Matt, thank you. I think I owe you about half a million dollars."

Matt laughed through his tears. "A little more than that, but we can work out logistics later." He pulled me close and kissed my cheek. "Thanks for being my twin. I love you, Kay."

"I love you too, Matt."

"I'll give you and 'Detective Babe' a minute," he said, half joking and half serious.

I watched him turn and buried my face into Lucas's shirt. "I just got you. I can't lose you."

He laid his head on top of mine. "You're not losing me, love. Can't get rid of me that easily."

My heart crumbled and fell to my shoes. I leaned back to look at his beautifully handsome face. "I'm so sorry you're in this mess. If I had just died like—"

"No," he cut me off, holding my face between his hands. "I don't care what brought us to this point. You are all I care about, Karissa. I choose this no matter what. I choose you every second of every day without a doubt, in a heartbeat. You are my choice."

With each one of his passionate words, I knew I could never deserve him. But through some twist of fate, he was mine. I was the luckiest girl in the world for that reason alone. "You are everything I ever wanted. You've been there for me in all my bad yesterdays, you're here today, and I swear to be there for you for the rest of forever."

"Karissa, *when* we get through this, will you marry me?"

I took a harsh breath in, standing in the middle of a cold concrete cell with nothing but pajamas and freezing bare feet. Coleman's and my blood had dried to my face, hair, and clothes. I could only imagine what a horrifying mess I looked like, and yet this boy, this perfect boy in a suit, had just asked me to be his wife. "Lucas…"

A grin took over his face. He patted his pockets and looked over his suit. Finally, he reached to his ankle and pulled a long thread from the slacks. He hunched over and tied a perfect knot in the piece of string. With a nervous grin, he held it up and whispered, "Karissa Sage Anderson, will you marry me?"

My heart fluttered. I couldn't believe it. Lucas Carter, *the Lucas Carter*, was asking me to marry him, to be his wife, to raise his kids, to grow old with him. It was my dream. "Yes," I said simply, forcing my voice to be steady. "Lucas, I want nothing other than this. Yes!"

He held my hand, lightly kissing the top of it as he slid the string around my finger. "I love you, Swan Lake."

"I love you, Detective Carter."

His arms wrapped themselves around my middle, his lips crashing into mine as he lifted me in the air and spun me around.

For one moment, a single brief moment, I forgot where we were. I forgot having the rest of my life was still questionable. I forgot Sienna existed. I forgot Coleman.

For a single brief moment, I was Karissa Anderson, fiancée of Lucas Carter, and that's all I needed.

As soon as my feet hit the ground, reality came smashing back.

"What about Taylor and Tyler?" Matt whimpered almost silently.

"And Drew," Lucas piped in, his hand sliding into mine.

"Drew?"

Lucas shook his head, rubbing his beard as he talked. "He was in the lobby. Coleman gave him some kind of shot. That's the last thing I saw before I passed out."

This was getting to be too much. Matt looked at me for rescuing us all. Lucas looked at me for answers. I couldn't do either. I was as trapped as they were.

Coleman was right, everyone I loved was in danger.

And it was all my fault.

"Taylor, Tyler, Drew, Mrs. Coleman," I muttered, raising my fingers as I counted.

The pieces fell together in my head like a puzzle. I backed into the wall, the room spinning. I swore, getting a good look out of Matt.

Lucas kept his hand tightly in mine, pinning me to reality. "What is it, babe? What's wrong?"

"The monsters," I whispered. "They are the monsters."

Matt gripped his head, pulling on his messy hair. "What are you saying?"

"Coleman turned the twins, Drew, and Mrs. Coleman into monsters," I forced out. "That's the game."

Lucas clenched his jaw, his eyes wide.

"It's cat and mouse."

CHAPTER 28

Lucas felt weightless as hands threw him out of the truck. It was a brief moment of flying before the ground came rushing up to meet him. He lay on the ground for only a moment before tossing his neck and throwing the black bag off his head. He tucked his hands under his shoe, moving his wrist up and down, creating friction between the zip ties holding his hands captive.

Finally, it snapped, and Lucas jumped to his feet. He brushed the dirt off his suit, slowly raising his head to see what horrors awaited him.

A rocky dirt path stretched out in front of him, sidled on either side by long dead corn stalks taller than his head. The path stopped short a few blocks ahead and cut to a corner. For as far as he could see, he was surrounded.

Lucas was in the middle of a maze.

"Ladies and gentlemen, boys and girls, it is my proud honor to welcome you to the first ever Coleman Corn Maze," Coleman's voice boomed across the field.

Lucas looked up as a camera whirred toward him, following his every movement.

"Not only is this the largest maze ever invented, but it is the first to be broadcast live across the entire world!" he said excitedly.

"Broadcast?" Lucas whispered to himself.

"That's right!" Coleman said as if he had heard Lucas. "With over 157 countries tuned in, we have the largest audience of all time. We are making history left and right. Now, of course, there are some rules."

HITTING THE GROUND RUNNING

The dark sky glittered with the number one.

Not only was Lucas trapped left and right, but even the sky was a trap. It was a dome, masking the night sky.

"Number one, no cutting through the corn, trust me you don't want to find out what happens if you try that," Coleman said with a laugh.

Lucas gently touched the corn, not surprised when it bounced back at him, matching his force.

The sky rolled over with the number two. "Second, the first person to make it to the end wins a life of fortune and fame. What happens to everyone else? You get to spend the rest of your short lives fighting to the death in the maze."

"Wonderful," Lucas muttered.

"And as a bonus round, the person with the most kills gets a shortcut out of the maze!"

Lucas thought through the people he knew he was trapped with. Not one of them would kill willingly. Why would Coleman add that if he knew they weren't going to even try?

"Also, because I'm so nice," he added, "I'd like to advise you to be a little extra quiet…or not. The people of the world want a show! Say hello!"

The sky transformed into a view of crowds gathered around screens, cheering as their faces appeared.

Coleman was right, the world was watching.

Now was the time to show them who Coleman really was.

It was time to show the world the truth.

Lucas took a cautious step forward, half expecting the ground to explode that instant. The air was chilly, almost cold. "Don't worry, Karissa," he said, looking up at the sky. "I'm coming."

In the dark cold moments, as he walked, his thoughts circled back to his mom. She had been there for him every day from the funeral to today. No matter how long he took to get back to her, or how many times he missed Sunday dinners, she was still his loving mom.

Regret was the one thing that had almost drowned him in the last two years. That was his breaking point.

From the moment he completed his mission, getting his girl back, he promised himself he wouldn't do that anymore. No more sleepless nights, no more letting anxiety ruin his life, no more regret.

He had to keep that promise, even now. His mom was safe, that's what mattered. He was going to get out of this and spend every Sunday with her.

Deep in his heart, he prayed she wasn't watching. He hoped she was still in her little house on the corner, planning craft nights for her friends.

A monstrous roar broke the silence, scaring Lucas so badly that he fell to the ground. The pebbles bounced.

Lucas cursed. The beast was coming.

He crouched in his starting position, the muscle memory of football coming back. He could only imagine what the "people of the world" were thinking as he crouched like the quarterback was born to be. The tips of his fingers brushed the ground, and he closed his eyes, running through the same routine he had thousands of times in high school.

"Lucas Owen Carter, run, dodge, slide, catch," he whispered, the words feeling the same even after all this time. "It's up to you now. You got this."

He took one more breath and sprinted as fast as humanly possible.

The monster was right at his heels, ready to bite at any second.

A scream ripped through the night, a genuinely horrifying scream. The wail came from Matt. Lucas kept running, only slightly changing his direction.

Only moments after Matt's cry came a bone-chilling familiar yell.

It was his girl's.

CHAPTER 29

Karissa

I folded my arms over my thin shirt, the freezing air nipping at my skin. With each step, a new rock, stick, or piece of the corn stalk would jab my bare feet.

Growing up, while all the other kids were eagerly ripping off their shoes to play in the backyard, I was the one doing anything to protect my feet. I was a dancer; my feet were my life. And now, in the middle of a dark maze, I could feel slivers cracking through the skin I had worked so hard to protect. I wanted to cry out in frustration, but Coleman's warning of silence rocked my core.

In the chaos of it all, all I wanted was a hot shower. My face was sticky, my hair was stiff, and my pajamas were crusty, all from the blood I had spilled only hours before. The way I looked had always been important to me; it determined my self-worth most days.

I guess that was exactly Coleman's idea here.

To rip my entire identity apart. To orchestrate the entire world to watch me in the worst state I've ever been in. To watch me die wearing another person's blood. He wanted me to die as the villain they all knew me as.

A thundering roar split the silence, shaking the corn stalks. Someone close by screamed, a genuinely horrifying scream.

I didn't waste another second. Ignoring the shooting pains in my feet, I sprinted down the path, keeping a few fingers at a time on the corn. Corners appeared out of nowhere, making me slide to a stop before continuing to run.

The wind whipped through my hair, my first breath of air since this whole night began. My arms were pumping, my feet barely kissing the dirt. The sound of my heartbeat pounded in my ears. I should've grown tired long ago, but the power deep inside kept the adrenaline flowing.

I turned a sharp corner. My foot caught a heavy lump on the ground, sending me flying off the path. My body hit the edge of the corn stalks but didn't let me through. It seized me, midair, for only a moment before throwing me back out onto the hard ground.

I felt like I had been electrocuted a thousand times. Steam was practically rising off me. "Coleman, you suck," I groaned, forcing myself to sit up.

The lump that sent me flying twitched. As gentle as possible, I inched toward it, trying to determine what it was in the darkness. My fingers traced it, shaking as they went. I could feel the untied shoes, the cuffed pants, the frayed T-shirt.

A light clicked on above me, shedding light onto the horror laying inches in front of me.

Screams fell out my lips before I could stop them.

Matt stretched out his hand. A long slice stretched across his stomach, spilling his organs. His dazed eyes searched for me as I shrieked. He blinked, his face contorted in pain. "Who's there?"

"M-Matt?" I scooted toward him, slowly. "What happened?"

"Karissa, it was a…a monster," he said in ragged breaths. "The mon…monster."

I looked at what I had on me to cover the blood pouring out of his wound. Nothing. My hands pulled his shirt down as far as it would go, and I used my own hands to cover the majority of it. "You're gonna be fine, Matt," I sobbed. "We just gotta keep pressure on it until it stops bleeding, okay?"

He put his own red hands over mine. "Karissa," he said softly.

I kissed the top of his fingers. "You're freezing, dude. Don't worry, soon we'll be home and in front of the fireplace."

"Karissa."

"I think the blood is slowing!" I lied. "It's looking better already."

He laid back, burying his face in his hands and wailing. "Karissa, please stop."

"Oh my gosh, Matt, you have to look up," I urged. "Look at the stars."

The sky was fake, Coleman had locked us in a fabricated nature. Regardless, the stars, no matter how phony they were, were stunning.

"Do you remember when Mom told us she was pregnant with the twins?" I said, pulling his hands away from his eyes. I laced my fingers in between his, keeping a finger on his wrist. His heart was slow and faint, but it still beat. "We decided to go to Cosmos Infinite that night, just the two of us. We climbed to the roof, almost dying under all that rotten wood."

I glanced at him as he nodded, his eyes not leaving the sky. "We didn't even talk about the babies," he continued. "We just sat under the stars. The moon was full, so full it lit up the museum like a streetlamp."

"You told me about your zombie books and how we were gonna write our own." I laughed through my tears.

He took a long breath. "We always hated the endings," he groaned, "that's why we wanted to write our own."

"I still want to," I said after a beat of silence. "I need to know how Jack Brooklyn gets out of the grasps of the *Running Corpse*."

"Let's do it," he whispered.

I brought his hand closer as the pulse was getting fainter. "Matt?"

Nothing.

"Matt!"

"I'm still here, Kay," he moaned. "I just need a minute, okay?"

"Okay."

A few too quiet moments passed, making my pulse quicken.

"Matt?"

He sighed. "Yes?"

"Do you hear that?"

A low growl sent chills down my spine.

"Karissa, holy—" He pushed himself to sit up, his eyes growing wide with terror. His finger lifted weakly.

Hesitantly, I turned, my breath catching in my throat as I saw *it*.

The beast towered over me three times. Its claws were as long as my leg. Its black eyes stretched up its slimy head, never blinking. It took a single step toward us, smiling with endless rows of teeth.

Matt and I cursed together.

"Karissa!" a voice from behind called. "Kari—"

I glanced over my shoulder, seeing Lucas skidding to a stop as soon as he caught sight of the creature. His eyes wandered from the beast to me, to Matt.

"Lucas," I whispered. "What do we do?"

He swallowed, looking between the three of us again.

The monster opened its enormous mouth, roaring so loud that the ground shook. It was ready to kill.

Matt squeezed my hand, diverting my attention. "Karissa, let me know if Jack Brooklyn makes it out."

I gave him a weird look. "We're gonna write it together, Matt. Jack Brooklyn was your idea."

He smiled sadly, squeezing my hand one more time. "He was *our* idea." He shoved me into the stalks, stunning me. In a single move, Matt threw himself to his feet, screamed in the monster's face, and took a few hobbling steps toward it.

"No!" I howled. Lucas caught the back of my shirt just as I tried to run. He pulled me back, wrapping his arms around my middle. I thrashed and scratched at him, doing anything to try to get out of his hold. "Let me go!" I shrieked at him. "Let me go, right now!"

His body shuddered with silent sobs.

The monster roared again.

I threw my feet back in an attempt to kick him. My body flailed wildly. Lucas didn't say anything, just tightened his grip on me.

"Let me go!"

The monster raised his hand.

"Drop me!"

It picked Matt up like a doll, snarling at him.

"Lucas, stop!"

Its other hand grabbed his upper body.

I fell completely still, terror filling my body like ice.

In an instant, the monster opened his arms, ripping Matt's body in half. The creature barely reacted. It simply dropped both pieces of my brother's body and wandered away.

Lucas loosened his hold on me. I fell pathetically to the ground, not knowing what to do. It felt like the stalks of corn were closing in on me. Everything was too confined. Vomit rose to my throat, threatening to come out. I was drenched in my sweat, but my core trembled. I was freezing and overheating all at once.

Lucas tucked his arms under my legs, sliding me onto his lap and holding me like a child. He didn't say anything. What could he say that would make sense in this moment?

For a long time, I just laid my head on his chest, shivering as beads of sweat dripped down my nose. The only sound was the wind brushing through the dead corn and the occasional scream of the beasts. Lucas stroked my cheek, his own body shaking in fear. His cheek rubbed my temple.

Merely feet away sat the corpse of my brother. I peeked out, stealing a glance at him, proving to myself this was real. Everything about him looked so horribly wrong.

That's when it hit me.

The complete shock turned into powerful wails, almost screams, of anguish. Tears streamed down my face, soaking Lucas's dress shirt in seconds. He brought me closer, softly crying with me.

"Shh," Lucas comforted me, holding a long kiss on my forehead. "It's okay, Karissa. It's okay, let it out."

I wanted to die.

I was the one that was supposed to die.

Matt was never supposed to die.

Hours went by, the sky never grew any lighter or darker. Lucas never gave up holding me and letting me sob endlessly into his chest. I cried the entire night.

It was only when the smell of death began to circle us that my emotions snapped.

In a flash, I went from being completely heartbroken, ready to give up and die, to rageful, vengeance filling my bones. My scars burned and ached, and power ripped its way down my arms. I looked up, the red glow from my eyes lit the path ahead of us.

It was time for Coleman to die.

Now.

I stood, getting a surprised look from Lucas. Once I was all the way up, I let my muscles contort to Sienna's liking. I spit on my hands, using them to wipe as much blood as possible off my face. Using my tippy-toes, I reached up to the top of a stalk and ripped the white security camera off it.

"Hey, Cole," I growled at the camera. "I know why you put us in here."

Lucas pushed himself to his feet, putting a hand on my shoulder. "Karissa, what are you doing?" he whisper-shouted.

I looked back at him, giving him a subtle look.

He didn't flinch as Sienna's eyes stared back at him.

"You're scared," I said, turning back to the camera. "You know you'll never be as powerful as us, and that scares you. You locked us here far away from you, trying to kill us while you're safe in your office."

"Karissa," he nudged me. "Why are you doing this? You're just egging him on."

I ignored him. "You locked us in here to give the people of the world a show, right? Well, let's give them a real show."

"Karissa, I need you to talk to me," Lucas said, his voice serious.

I dropped the camera, pulling him as close as I could. "I'm gonna end this, Lucas. Once and for all."

He brushed my hair back. "Love, you just had quite possibly the worst night of your life. Are you sure this is what we should do next? What if we just make our way out of the maze?"

"Then what happens?" I countered. "Coleman lives and torments us for the rest of our lives? We can't play his games anymore."

"You know I love you, right?" he said with a small smile.

I put my hands on his cheeks, planting a long, deep kiss on his lips. "I love you, Lucas, that's why I'm doing this."

Lucas's eyes were tight, ready to continue talking me out of all this, but he just nodded.

I picked the forgotten camera off the ground and raised it. "You and me, one-on-one fight." I gritted my teeth. "Get us out of here and fight me like a man."

A sharp scratching noise interrupted me.

Lucas and I whipped around, adrenaline firing through our systems. Three of the giant monsters stood only feet in front of us, arms raised, ready to rip us apart at any second. The largest of the three lowered its face, its tooth brushing my cheek. I whimpered and tightly closed my mouth.

"That's quite enough, darling," a silky voice instructed. The monsters parted and backed up, letting the esteemed Dr. Coleman walk through. They simply watched him, not making any move to attack. "Aren't they beautiful?" he said casually. "Only a week ago they were uncontrollable. Now, with a few simple alterations to their DNA, they will listen to every word I say."

Lucas's hand slipped into mine.

He put his hand on the back of the largest one. "I call them Rifkins. Once a fatal mistake of the Minefield turned into one of my proudest creations." Coleman sighed happily and shot me a grin. "I like your proposition, Karissa."

"Oh?" I said, forcing myself to be as casual as him.

"Yes, you're right. I wanted to give the world a show, but I was missing a crucial piece," he said.

"And what's that?" Lucas piped in.

"The boss level," he rubbed his hands together, excitedly.

"Boss level?"

He paced the small path, not able to contain his happiness. "You see, in every video game, the so-called 'boss' is the hardest character to be defeated at the very end of the story. It's the resolution, the proof that the protagonist has completed its quest."

I cocked my head, it was working, and he was taking my bait.

"You and me, sweetheart," Coleman beamed. "The boss level."

CHAPTER 30

The next few hours were a blur.

Once Coleman had accepted my challenge, he called his workers to pick us up. The corn stalks blew furiously under the helicopter wind. Lucas climbed up first, making sure it was legit before calling me to follow.

I looked back at Coleman, sincerity in my eyes. "If I lose, I need you to promise me you'll let Lucas go."

He tilted his head, his hands still laced perfectly behind his back. "And how do you know I'll keep my promise? You'll be dead."

My voice screamed to rip his head off, but I shook it away. "Because I know you, Cole. You're a lot of things, but you're a man of your word till the very end."

"Ah, sweetheart," he said with a sickening smile. "I promise, if Lucas doesn't interfere with me or any of my plans, I'll leave him alone. He'll be safe from me."

I climbed the rope ladder.

Lucas reached down and pulled me in, his eyes on Coleman, following just behind. "You okay?" he shouted over the roar of the wind.

"I will be!" I yelled back. "You?"

He kissed my hand, smiling at the thread still wrapped around my finger. "I'm okay."

Together, we sat side by side, watching the world grow smaller as we flew.

We shared a look as the full view of the maze came into view.

The property stretched over hundreds of acres, with thousands of twists and turns. The complete labyrinth was full of dead ends, trap doors, and an ending so small you would miss it if you blinked, there was no surviving it.

We landed in the middle of Coleman Labs. The sight of the buildings brought a sinking feeling to my stomach.

For the first time since I had this idea, I wondered if it was a good idea. There were only two ways it would end.

It was the only chance we had.

His guards jumped out first, surrounding us before we could even think about running.

Coleman walked behind us as nonchalantly as a morning stroll.

Cameras whirred as they pointed at us. The world was still watching our every move.

Good.

We were led to the main suite, the place where it had all started.

The usual doctors were there, waiting for us, along with a numerous group of women holding beauty supplies. They instructed us to lie on the white tables.

I stared at the table, the lump in my throat stretching. This was where I had spent two years. Two years of unimaginable pain, guilt, and misery.

And here I was, willingly.

I could feel Lucas's gaze steady on me, and I gathered my courage. He had to believe I was confident in my plan. Regardless, he was going to be safe, that's all that mattered.

I climbed onto the table, hoping Lucas would do the same.

The girls closed the curtain between us.

I flinched as the cold water hit my body. The ladies tugged at my ruined clothes as they snipped them off. Their fingernails dug into my hair, the smell of strong soap filling the air. I cringed as they pulled the splinters out of my feet with their sharp tweezers.

I felt stupidly vulnerable, laying on that table as the women washed me from head to toe.

"What are you doing?"

One of the girls leaned over me, her long hair tickling my face. "Admiral Coleman wanted you to look beautiful for your finale."

Once they were satisfied with their cleaning, they sat me up and handed me a pair of black clothes. I pulled them on, finally feeling human again.

I looked in the full-length mirror across from my table.

My hair was curled and draped down my back. My face was freshly plastered with heavy dark makeup. The wardrobe I was given was just another one of Coleman's jokes. Stretchy black clothes with a matching shawl that fell to the floor, and sharp heels, of course, completed the ensemble.

He had dressed me like Sienna.

He had dressed me to be the villain.

The curtain swung open.

Lucas sat on the edge of the table, wearing nothing but dark shorts. He looked at me, an empty look in his eyes. He clenched his jaw, his words sitting on the tip of his tongue.

I put my hands on his cheeks, pressing my forehead against his. "Still here, Detective?"

He put his hands over mine. "Still here, Swan Lake." His gaze caught mine. "Are you sure about this?"

"I have to be," I whispered back.

"It's time," one of the doctors interrupted.

I tilted Lucas's head up, pulling him in for what could very well be our last kiss. He pulled me closer, his lips lingering between kisses. He could feel it.

"Now," the doctor urged.

Taking a long breath, I released myself. "I love you."

"I love you too," he said quietly. "But, hey, I'll see you after this, right? Maybe we could go see a movie or something? Seven?"

"Absolutely," I laughed sadly.

"Awesome," he replied, his voice thick with emotion. "See you then, Karissa."

He was led out of the room, his head craning over his neck to look back at me until the very last second.

It was my turn.

HITTING THE GROUND RUNNING

The doctor opened the door for me, his hand wrapped tightly around his gun. We walked in silence down the never-ending halls. My heart lurched to my throat as I recognized the path we were taking.

He stopped in front of the entry, pulling his card out. "Hey, Sienna?"

I blinked out of my thoughts. "It's Karissa, Doctor."

"Karissa, I'm Dr. Peck" he started again, "give him hell."

His words surprised me. He looked as if he was ready to kill Coleman himself. I gave him an encouraging nod. "You got it."

We sighed together as he opened the door. The locks clicked and hissed as we entered. We were in the middle of the arena, the room where I had claimed my very first victim.

The thousands of seats were now completely filled. The room was alive with nervous energy. The audience roared, cheering and booing as the doors opened.

"Please welcome, our master of ceremonies, the man who made this all possible, Adm. Cole Coleman!" the announcer boomed.

Coleman walked in the door across from mine, white fog swirling around his feet. The room screamed in excitement. He waved, shooting a finger gun in my direction. Dressed in all white, he made himself the hero.

Fine.

He wants to make me the villain. That's just fine.

"And, of course, the heartbreaker from the suburbs, kid killer, mass murderer, and the reason we all live in fear, Sienna!"

Gee, thanks.

The crowd booed viciously, practically hissing as black fog circled my ankles. The bouncy floor sunk my heel the moment I stepped through. I kicked off my heels and strutted to the middle of the floor.

"Where's Lucas?" I demanded as soon as Coleman and I were face-to-face.

He tossed his neck, gesturing toward Lucas tied up beside Dr. Peck. "Don't worry," he said, nudging my shoulder, "I'm just making sure he's not getting in my way, right?"

I thought of our deal and simply nodded. "Let's do this."

"One moment." He turned to the crowd. "Wouldn't this be a better show if this was a fair fight?"

The audience cheered in agreement.

"Don't you, Sienna?"

I squinted at him.

"I think so." He lifted a syringe, making my stomach drop to my toes.

The red liquid stared back at me, taunting me.

He raised the syringe to his neck and plunged the thick serum in. He leaned back, screaming toward the roof as the Minefield overtook his body. His body contorted, scars erupted across his body, and his eyes turned bright red. Once the Minefield was completely through his system, he straightened his posture and nodded contently. "That's much better."

The crowd clapped in delight.

"Dr. Thompson, if you would," he directed.

The world was watching.

Coleman was now Minefield subject twenty-nine.

It was an even fight.

One of us wouldn't leave the mat.

A bell chimed.

And it began.

Coleman started strong, lunging toward me, his fists raised.

I dodged his first attack, diving to the side. With a spin, I kicked his abdomen and punched his beady little eye. I bounced on my feet, refusing to lose my momentum.

He laughed, his mouth open wide. "Is that all you got? Some playground punches and a gut-buster? That's why poor little Matty is dead."

I snarled, ripping my shawl off my bare shoulders. "Good one."

He chuckled. "While we're on the subject of your siblings, you'll never guess where sweet little Taylor and Tyler are."

There was nothing he could say that would surprise me.

"They're living a wonderful life of life-sucking beasts I like to call Rifkins. In fact, guess which one ended up killing Matty! Innocent sweet little Taylor."

Except that.

Angry tears slipped out, spreading the jet-black makeup down my cheeks. With a rageful scream, I ran forward, tackling Coleman. Using all my weight, I held his wrists down with my hands, digging my knee into his stomach.

"You're good," he grinned, "but I'm better."

Before I could comprehend what was happening, Coleman flipped me over onto the ground. He loomed over me, his sardonic smile still stuck on his pale face. Needing only a single hand to constrain both of mine, he used the other to squeeze my throat.

My scars burned with rage. I could feel the burn from my penetrating stare. "You-you're going to pay for everything," I pushed out.

He giggled like a maniac. "I have worked my whole life for the sake of humanity. There's no payment, my dear." His voice was soft and sweet as his grip got tighter.

My lungs burned. Panic rose in my chest, swelling and pounding in my rib cage. The world blurred around me. I tilted my neck, getting a glimpse of Lucas fighting his restraints.

The crowd boomed, shaking the room with their voices.

My eyelids fluttered, the heavy eyelashes catching my hair. "No mercy," I mouthed, giving myself a boost of encouragement.

He glared back.

I thrashed and flailed, doing anything to get a single breath of air in. I kicked his back as hard as I could, struggling to keep my energy up. I wrapped my freshly manicured nails around his wrist, digging them into his skin. I screamed in his face, putting every ounce of energy into digging my sharp nails until I felt his solid bones. With a quick flick of my finger, I snapped each tendon in his tight wrist. His body shook as he absorbed his own pain.

I thrashed once more, throwing him off balance for a split second, but that's all I needed. I tucked my legs through his and pressed my feet against his chest, bending my knees and launching him across the mat.

Air flooded my lungs. I coughed, the quick breaths aching my throat. I took shallow breaths, trying to remember how to breathe properly. "You killed him," I said with a raspy voice. I stood, feeling the marks from his fingers on my neck. "You killed my brother!"

Sienna was coming fast, and this time, I relaxed my own identity and let her.

I stormed across the mat, picking up Coleman and throwing him back onto the ground. Pure strength filled my body. I threw my legs over him, slamming my fist down on his face as I forced my knees into his ribs, snapping them.

Coleman gasped, his face pale with pain. I continued beating him, just as I did in the lobby. Without an ounce of hesitation, I punched him. Over and over again, I threw my fist into his evil broken face. With each blow, my hand was drenched in more blood, but I didn't stop.

A sharp stab hit my side. I yelped and stopped for only a moment, looking down to see what he had done.

A syringe sat, stuck in my hip, its white liquid emptying into my veins.

Sienna's power was leaving, like blood draining from a body.

He had played dirty.

He had made himself a part of Minefield and taken mine.

I slipped off Coleman, landing pathetically on my back beside him. I ripped at my chest, trying to tear my burning heart out. My eyes felt like they were going to pop out of the socket. I looked at my arms, almost expecting my scars to be on fire as they got darker and sunk deeper into my skin.

Then every ounce of energy was gone in a flash.

I was barely able to breathe, my reactions were slow, and my vision was glitchy.

Coleman knelt beside me and spit blood onto my face. "No mercy," he mocked me, raising his fist and throwing it down. Without any hesitation, he punched me. Over and over again, he threw his fist into my defenseless broken face. With each blow, his hand was drenched in more blood, but he didn't stop.

Death was so close I could practically touch it.

He raised his fist for one final punch and was tackled to the ground.

I rolled over, my mouth full of warm metallic blood.

Lucas was holding Dr. Coleman down with every bit of force he had. I twisted my neck, seeing Dr. Peck holding Lucas's abandoned ropes.

The world was mushy and thick.

"Karissa!" Lucas cried.

Coleman was too powerful for Lucas; I had to help him. I tucked my elbow underneath myself, forcing myself to stay conscious. Beside me, I could hear Lucas and Coleman beating each other.

Coleman caught my eye and sent his foot flying, hitting me right in the chest. I flew into the wall, bouncing off it and rolling to a permanent stop.

Every bone in my body felt shattered. I felt like a skin sack of bone shards.

"We could have had it all, Karissa!" Coleman roared. "All you had to do was follow a few simple orders."

"Lucas," I moaned.

"This is all your fault!"

"No." I wasn't sure if the word made it past my lips.

"*This* is just for you, Sienna."

A sickening snap made the entire room fall silent. Lucas's body fell next to me. His eyes half open, his arms behind his back, and his neck…his neck.

Everything about it was…wrong.

The doors to the gym blew off the hinges. The crowd screamed. Thousands of armed soldiers swarmed the arena. Their words bounced around my head, not a syllable making any sense. They were shouting orders, gunshots echoed off the walls.

"Karissa," a southern voice urged. He looked so familiar, but I didn't have the energy to remember why. "Come on, it's okay, it's okay," he promised, his tone not agreeing with his words. "We're getting you out of here. You're safe now."

As I lay on the mat, my entire life ran in circles through my head.

For the first time in two years, I thought of Amber, my friend. I thought of Jonathan, Lucas's best friend. I thought of Dad and

Madame Roussel. I thought of working at Joanna's Diner with Tony. I thought of my family. I thought of Mom working until her feet bled. Matt picked up whatever job he could to keep a roof over our heads. He had given up his true passion to keep us safe. Tyler wanted nothing more than to be the best football player ever; he had the mindset to go pro at eight years old. Taylor didn't just have the desire to dance, she had the drive. She was willing to do anything to dance forever.

I thought of my future.

Lucas, the boy of my dreams, had asked me to be his wife only hours earlier. I could practically see a two-story house, with a porch that stretched all the way around. Our kids would run our lives, and we would love it. He would've been the perfect dad and perfect husband.

The chief's final words ripped every thought out of my head in an instant.

"Coleman's dead."

The End